D0350684

Samphire Song

JILL HUCKLESBY

Albert Whitman & Company
Chicago, Illinois

Library of Congress Cataloging-in-Publication Data

Hucklesby, Jill.
Samphire song / by Jill Hucklesby.
pages cm
Summary: Fourteen-year-old Jodie, a geeky loner dealing with
family problems, forges a bond with her new horse, Samphire,
but must find and rescue him when he goes missing.
ISBN 978-0-8075-7224-5
[1. Horses—Fiction. 2. Family problems—Fiction.] I. Title.
PZ7.H86367Sam 2013
[Fic]—dc23
2012031821

For more information about Albert Whitman & Company,
visit our web site at www.albertwhitman.com.

*With special thanks to Becky Hucklesby
and Sophie Adshead*

Chapter One

Hooves thundering on sand, across the wide sweep of the sun-washed bay. Salt-spray splashing up, stinging our eyes, matting our hair. The taste of the ocean on our tongues and the cry of gulls in our ears. Faces forward, almost nestling in warm manes. Knees gripping leather, feet taut in stirrups, bodies carried by an energy surge, like surfers balancing on boards, rushing at breakneck speed to shore.

We're riding into the warm July wind and my cheeks are streaming with tears, whipped up by the whoosh of air against lashes. I'm breathing in blue sky mixed with the muskiness of horse sweat. My heart feels like it's dancing to the deep *dada da dum* rhythm beneath my feet. Laughter hiccups from my throat.

I'm looking at Dad, who is focusing straight

ahead, brow furrowed in concentration. Now he's glancing at me and a massive smile is radiating from his mouth, causing creases to fan from the edges of his blue eyes.

"Yeeha!" he calls. "Last one to the rock is a bandit..." He's lengthening his reins and urging Kaloo, a retired racehorse who is the fastest mount at the stables, to gallop to victory.

"In your dreams," I yell back, asking Rambo, my favorite chestnut, to pick up the pace. He responds willingly, eager to please. I curl down farther on his neck, jockey style, trying to make us more aerodynamic. Kaloo takes off like a rocket, with Dad almost clinging to the curve of his arched neck. Dad usually rides like a cowboy, laid back in the saddle, but now, slumped forward, he looks more like a highwayman, fleeing for his life.

"Hey, tough guy, what are you waiting for?" I whisper toward Rambo's ears, which flick back and forth like furry antennae.

And as my calves brush his belly gently, we push forward in pursuit of Kaloo's impressive black tail, which is flying behind him regally. Lumps of wet sand splatter onto my nose and eyelids as our competitors veer a little to the left, directly ahead of us.

Rambo grunts and instinctively changes course, his feet following a deeper gully where the tide is oozing its way back in. His hooves smash down on the water like marbles clattering onto glass.

At fourteen hands, Rambo is struggling to gain ground against Kaloo, the mighty seventeen-hand colossus. But I can tell Kaloo is beginning to tire under the two-hundred pound weight around his neck and on his shoulders, and his pace is changing. His long, graceful legs are slowing to a comfortable canter, despite Dad's protestations and offers of extra carrots for supper.

I'm pulling my hat farther down to protect my eyes as a barrage of shingle-studded ocean mud is propelled from Kaloo's hooves in our direction.

We're narrowing the gap and Rambo is holding his head steady and proud, without interference from me on the bit. I'm willing him on with every fiber of my being and it feels as if we're moving in perfect synchronicity.

Dad and Kaloo are close now, surrounded by salt mist. I can hear Dad calling me, his voice full of exhilaration and mock panic.

"Jodie...Jo-die..."

And the water vapor is enveloping him, blurring rider and horse into a silhouette, a mirage as faint as a memory.

"Jodie!" I jump at the sound of my name, coming from behind me. When I turn, I see the face of Rachel Holmes in the space above the half-closed loose-box door. As my mind tries to make the leap from past to present, a shudder ripples down my spine.

"Are you OK?" Rachel asks.

"Yeah," I nod. "I'm good, thanks," and I thrust my fork into the pile of hay at my feet with surprising force.

Rachel, at sixteen, is the oldest of the volunteers who help out at Whitehawk Farm Stables in return for free riding and lessons. She tries to keep a team spirit going, encouraging us to eat our packed lunches on hay bales in the yard in summer or upstairs in the sand school in winter. Lunchtimes are legendary for the swapping of pony gossip and funny stories. I listen in sometimes, on the periphery of the circle. I don't want to talk, though. I come here to *not* talk.

I prefer to be around the horses, keeping busy, mucking out, cleaning tack, getting things done. It helps me forget and helps me remember.

"Can you do Jiminy's box with me after this?" Rachel asks. I nod and smile. I know she's trying to be a friend and give me the chance to loosen up. But that's like asking Tutankhamun to open his own tomb. What would I say? That I miss my dad more than words can express? That my little brother, Ed, has kidney disease and Mom and I are worried sick?

Joyce, the bereavement counselor who used to visit,

says that people are like animals. When we're wounded, we sometimes try to isolate ourselves from further harm. Animals look for a piece of high ground, a tall tree, or a deep burrow. Mom, Ed, and I feel like we've been shipwrecked on an island. Joyce says, in time, we'll build our own life raft. (Mom says she hopes we'll be rescued by Johnny Depp, but only if he's wearing his pirate costume.)

Horses, on the other hand, don't want explanations. Just care and respect. That's fine by me. When I look into their eyes, I can tell their life story. I can see whether there is trust or fear, playfulness or anger. Many have had several owners and homes. They all have different personalities. But they have one big thing in common—their destiny isn't their choice.

They know a thing or two about survival. They're very intuitive. And I'm sure they understand people very well. Unlike the girls here who think I'm just a geeky loner with "family problems," the horses make no judgement and accept me as I am.

I wonder if they read the story in *my* eyes? If they do, they'll see that I'm Jodie Palmer. I'm fourteen years old. And I have a rock where my heart should be.

Chapter Two

"Hey, Sticko," says Ed, a bit breathlessly, raising a hand from the bar of his exercise bike and waving at me. He calls me Stick because, although I'm nearly five feet seven inches tall, I don't have any curves, no matter which angle you see me from. Even my nose is straight, like a Roman soldier's. Mom prefers to describe me as "athletic" and says that my shape will develop "all in good time." Until then, Ed says, I'm in danger of being mistaken for a bookmark and squashed into one of Mom's Jane Austen novels for all eternity.

"Hey, Teddy," I respond, yawning. This is my family's pet name for Ed, who was, until his kidney troubles, quite squishy in the tummy department. "Mom says dinner's ready and you have to wash your hands before you come to the table."

"You're always on my case," he complains, waving his arms theatrically, looking as if he's just crossed the line in the Tour de France.

"Just relaying orders," I tell him. "How was vampire club?"

"They sucked and they sucked until my blood ran dry!" he gasps, pulling his face into a grimace, then stumbling off the bike and lurching toward me like a monster. I put my hand on his head so he can't move. He looks up at me sweetly through his long, blond bangs.

"It didn't taste so good though, so they decided to give it back." He grins, looking just like Dad, blue eyes twinkling. A sensation approaching pain shoots across my chest. I put my arms round Ed and squeeze, not too hard. He hugs me back. He feels clammy after his exercise, which he has to do every evening to help his body rid itself of the toxins that his struggling kidneys can't deal with.

Ed isn't quite eleven yet and he's really brave. He has to go to dialysis three times a week at the hospital, to have his blood cleaned up. It's taken out through a tube in his arm, filtered to remove waste products, and returned by another tube. The whole process lasts four hours, which means Ed misses a lot of school. He says this is one good thing about having sketchy kidneys. He doesn't fall behind, though, because he has a brilliant teacher named Miss Snow who coordinates his make-up work. To Ed, she is "the Evil Ice-Woman."

"One day, global warming will melt her and she'll stop putting math prep in my cubbyhole," he says darkly.

I'm looking at Ed's floor, which is covered with small bits of dark plastic, laid out in shape order. He follows my gaze.

"It's a stealth bomber," he says, almost reverently. I don't get his thing about making model airplanes, just as he doesn't get my thing about horses.

"Wow, a stealth bomber," I reply.

"It's not just a stealth bomber, actually," he states.

"It's a B-2 Spirit and I've been waiting for it for two months."

"That's nice," I say, ruffling his shaggy mop. His bedroom already looks like an aircraft museum. My chest tightens again as I imagine how Dad, who was an air force pilot, would have loved it.

"I don't diss you for wanting to shovel up poo all day long, Whinny," he points out. Whinny is his other nickname for me, when he wants to hit below the belt.

"Yeah you do," I say. His expression changes from a petulant frown to a big grin. I feel mine doing the same, even though I'm trying to keep a straight face. Ed's smiles are impossible to resist. Even the fiercest doctors at the hospital are won over by his charms and end up chuckling.

"What's for dinner?" he asks warily. Mom is an erratic cook. If there isn't a plan, she'll invent a dish out of whatever's in the fridge, so you can end up with pea and baked-bean pasta or spaghetti risotto. Ed has to have a special diet, avoiding food with lots of potassium, like bananas, tomato sauces, and melons. We try to sit down together on a Sunday and make a list of meals for the following week but the trouble is, none of us likes being organized. Dad was the planner in the family. Everything used to run like clockwork. Even when Ed got sick three years ago and started his regular hospital trips, daily life ticked along and everyone smiled.

That seems like a long time ago.

"Veggie lasagna," I reply. Ed makes a face. "It's OK, it's the one I helped her make last week and we froze it, remember?"

"No cauliflower?" he shudders.

"No," I confirm. "Only the leftover beetroot."

Ed squirms and hugs his body protectively. "Yeeeuch!" he splutters.

"You're too easy to wind up, Teddy," I tell him, grinning, taking his hand and pulling him onto the landing.

"You are both in league with the Evil Ice-Woman.

You just want to make my life a misery. Good-bye," he announces, swinging his leg over the wooden banister rail and sliding down to the bottom.

"I'm your big sis, it's my job," I call after him. My eyes rest on the framed family photos filling the long wall on my right. Shots of Mom and Dad when they were young (one of Dad on a bike is the spitting image of Ed); a close-up of them on their wedding day, outside city hall, with a caption that reads "Ali and Mike got married!" (It's the card they sent to all the surprised relatives after the event). Then there's Mom with her sister, Auntie Connie, who runs a pet rescue sanctuary; me as a baby in an embarrassing hat and no top; Dad and his parents, the day he got his "wings." The biggest one is of the four of us in our fancy clothes and neat hair against a blue background in a cheesy studio setup.

Underneath this is my favorite; Dad and me riding in North Wales on vacation when I was eight, the first time we'd gone on a ride together. He'd sung a Welsh song about "yonder green valleys" in a very loud voice even though I pleaded with him to shut up. Even the sheep who heard it ran away, bleating angrily.

The sound of running water from the downstairs bathroom brings me back to earth. My eyes open to see Ed, at the bottom of the stairs, showing me his freshly washed hands.

"Very nice," I say, walking downstairs toward him. "Now go and turn the water off."

Ed obliges then asks, "Are we going in, squadron leader?" before we open the kitchen door.

"Affirmative," I answer. We shake hands. Ed turns the round handle and pushes.

We're met by two unusual sights—a room full of bubbles and lit candles, and Mom, beaming, serving up a fantastic smelling dish, with our favorite garlic doughballs. The transparent, soapy globes drift and pop on work surfaces, the fridge, the floor, and even our noses. Ed runs around, clapping his hands on as many as he can get to.

"Change of plan," Mom announces. "There was squash in the fridge, so I've made a bubbling soup!"

Chapter Three

Mom, whose hair is usually pinned up in a messy bun, is pushing loose, wavy blonde wisps behind her ear, the way she does when she's about to announce something important. She is also frowning at Ed, whose tongue is poised above his plate, ready to lick up what's left of his dinner.

"Uh-uh," warns Mom.

"D'oh," says Ed, flashing her a smile so radiant it seems to light up the room and envelop us all. That's how it used to be with Dad, too—women seemed to crumble in the presence of that grin. Ed even bought him a mug for what turned out to be our last family Christmas, with "Babe Magnet" on it. Mom pretended to be outraged. Dad was quite pleased.

Mom's sternness has vanished and she is beaming back at Ed. "I have some good news," she begins.

"Stick's moving in at the stables so I can have her room?" Ed suggests, clapping his hands.

"You are never, ever going to have my room, Teddy. Get used to it," I tell him. He makes a devastated face and drops his head onto his arms on the table with a thud.

Mom looks at me, her eyes daring me to guess the mystery. I suddenly have a horrible thought and I can feel my eyebrows knitting together, the way they do when I'm confronted with a huge obstacle, like an English essay.

"You've got a boyfriend," I state, my voice flat and dull.

"No!" Mom laughs.

"You do talk to that Rubber Gloves quite a lot," says Ed, resting his chin on his hand.

"He's my editor," responds Mom gently. "We discuss gardening things." It may be a trick of the light, but I think she's blushing a little. Mom's colleague got his nickname after Ed took a phone message one day and scribbled down his version of Rupert Glover.

"It's something nice that concerns all of us," says Mom.

"We've inherited money from a wrinkly old aunt we never knew we had?" suggests Ed.

"You're getting warm," teases Mom.

"We are the love children of an aging rock star who has finally claimed us and wants to give us a million dollars?" I ask.

"Not quite," answers Mom cryptically. Ed and I are both mulling this over when she finally relents.

"I've been offered a column in *Gardening Guru*. It's the first time I've had my very own space to fill every week. I'll be answering readers' questions and giving advice. And the money's really good," she adds in a whisper.

"That's so amazing," say Ed and I, in unison. We rush round the table and give her a big squeeze, which makes her giggle. Since Dad died, Mom has struggled to find enough freelance gardening writing. I know she worries a lot about the lack of money coming in. The huge smile on her face looks like a mixture of excitement and relief.

"I'll need to go to London two days a week," she explains, gauging our reaction.

"That's cool," says Ed. "We can take care of things here." Mom and I exchange glances. Ed sounds so grown up these days.

"The job's just the first part of the surprise, though," says Mom, as Ed and I sit down again. He narrows his eyes like a detective discovering a new, important clue.

"I'd like to treat you both to something special to celebrate," Mom adds more quietly. Her eyes look shiny in the candlelight. "Something from Dad and me."

I look at Ed. His mouth has formed into a silent "O" and now he's quietly chanting "Remote-controlled plane." My heart has started to beat quite loudly in my chest. I swallow hard, trying to suppress the rising hope that is surging up my body. Something I had believed impossible, something I have dreamed of since I was small, is coming into focus; a wish that is so big, even Santa couldn't come up with the goods.

A horse of my own!

I'm looking at Mom and she is nodding, reading my mind, and before I know it, I'm rushing back around the table to hug her, forcing back a deluge of hot, happy tears.

"Thank you," I manage to say, even though my throat is tight.

Mom holds me and reaches out a hand to Ed.

"I'm really happy for you, Stick," he says, his face serious. "It's the miracle we've been waiting for. A face transplant will change your life."

I pick up Mom's uneaten roll and throw it at him. Where annoying brothers are concerned, whole wheat is much better than white, carrying more weight and wounding capacity. Ed takes the blow on the head and flops back in his chair.

"Shut up, idiot," I say, laughter unexpectedly bubbling up through my voice.

"Brown bread," he croaks, and plays dead.

Chapter Four

I can't sleep. Through the night, strong March winds have been whirling around the house, moaning and rattling the windows. I'm snug under my duvet, almost mummified, lying straight and still, eyes wide open, thinking about Mom's promise. Ripples of excitement have been moving up and down my spine for the past five hours, mini waves with white horses on the top.

I've always loved white horses the best, ever since Dad won me a cute model one on the pier by shooting ducks in a row. I named him Al because he was an albino with pink eyes—a bit odd, when you come to think of it. He lives on my bookcase now, next to my framed photo of Dad and me on our Welsh riding trip.

There is a creaking sound, the unmistakable noise of

footsteps on our warped landing floorboards. The handle of my door is turning, ever so slowly. Despite being famously frightened of horror films and things that go bump in the night, I don't even hold my breath. In fact, I've been expecting a visit.

"Stick, are you awake?" The voice is small and hushed. I can just make out the weird shape of my brother, in his oversized Spider-Man pajamas, in the doorway.

"Yeah," I tell him. At this, he launches himself at my bed and snuggles in next to me, his teeth chattering.

"Aagh, your feet are really cold!" I exclaim.

"I've been doing stuff to the bomber," he tells me. Ed has trouble sleeping, but is quite happy to work on his model planes until tiredness overtakes him. Mom and I often find him on the floor in the morning, covered in glue and fuselage parts, snoring.

"Didn't you go to sleep at all?" I ask him.

"Nooooooooo," he sings, a high soprano.

"Shh, Teddy, you'll wake Mom up." I nudge him in the ribs, gently. "Me neither," I say. We grin at each other.

"Stick?"

"What?"

He motions for me to pull the duvet over our heads, so he can tell me something important. I'm reluctant to do this because before I can escape, he normally does something gross and smelly.

"I'm getting a remote-controlled model *plane*!" my brother squeals, making a drum roll in the bed with his feet.

"And I'm going to find the most beautiful horse in the world," I whisper. It feels good to say the words out loud in the dark. It's like announcing it to the universe.

"Wish Dad could come and help me choose," says Ed, matter-of-factly. Ed often refers to Dad as if he's away on a tour of duty and will be back soon.

"Me too." We're both silent for a few moments. Then Ed scratches his thigh and his elbow digs into me. I push it away, he forces it back. We have a contest for about twenty seconds and then give up and lie still again.

"Mine's a better present," Ed states.

"How do you figure?" I yawn, getting sleepy now.

"I don't have to feed it, brush it, or clean up its poo. And I won't need to do a thousand jobs to earn extra money to pay for its shoes and hairdresser," he tells me, holding his nose, making gestures that indicate my breath smells.

"Horses don't go to the hairdresser, idiot," I reply, huffing extra hard on him.

"Who does all those braid things, then?" he asks, yawning too.

"Their owners, usually."

"You don't even brush your own hair," he says, voice trailing away.

I'm about to remind Ed that running his fingers once every morning through his own scarecrow tufts doesn't count as a personal best in the style department when I see that his eyes are closed and his mouth slightly open. His breathing is regular and deep. He's in dreamland, probably with his remote-controlled plane, making it do loop-the-loops, thoughts of hospitals, tubes, and sketchy kidneys wiped from his memory.

"Sleep well, Teddy," I whisper, folding the duvet back, allowing cool, early-morning air to ripple over us.

Chapter Five

I'm waiting at the end of our lane for the school bus. Ed is going to the hospital for dialysis today so I'm alone, except for a New Forest pony and a donkey grazing on the green opposite me.

It's nice that animals roam where they please here. I often wonder how their owners find them to check their health, or to sell them at one of the regular auctions. It must be a massive game of hide-and-seek, but even the cleverest horse will be discovered in the end; the New Forest is contained by cattle grids and gates on its boundaries.

There's a low mist meandering across the dewy grass. The animals' breath mingles with it and it looks like they're standing on clouds.

A rumble to my right tells me that my bus is arriving. My classmates' faces are pressed against the glass, making them look like weird gargoyles. As the door flings open, a wave of harsh sound rushes out into the still morning. It hits my ears like small fists.

"Morning," says Bill, the driver, cheerily. "All aboard for Disneyland."

He says this every day with a big, toothy smile. My school, although rated "good" in the annual rankings, is about as far from the Magic Kingdom as Iceland is from the Sahara Desert.

"Morning," I reply, my eyes already scanning to see where the "safe" seats are: the ones least likely to be in the firing line of Niall Taylor and his crew, who practice their throwing skills (anything from pens to packed lunches) from their regular places at the back. Susie Price and her friends, the "Glossies," are also to be avoided. They think speaking while applying mascara counts as multitasking and reading celebrity magazines is the same as studying English. Ed calls them the

"Flossies" because they all wear braces in the hope of achieving a Hollywood smile.

As usual, there's an empty space next to Poppy Brill, who suffers from eczema and whose facial skin is deep red. She's in my year and, like me, keeps to herself. Her lips are moving to some song on her iPod and she's staring out of the steamed-up window, a slender hand tapping out the beat on her knee.

When I sit next to her, she glances at me and gives me a fleeting smile. I nod in acknowledgement and put my bag on my lap, like body armor. I'm wishing that Ed was here, even though he is annoyingly bubbly and talkative early in the morning. Having him around, until he gets dropped off at the grade school, makes the journey go quicker and means I don't get the chance to drift away into daydreams, which usually involve Dad and me galloping along the shore. It's such a hard place to return from, and sometimes I have to shut myself in the restroom before homeroom just to get a grip so that I don't explode when girls like

Alice Hebden and Sarah Sparks discuss nail polish or designer jeans like they're the most important things in the world.

Lessons are OK, especially math and science, but I'm happiest at the stables or at home with Mom and Ed. But now I have something amazing to think about—something that will help me get through the school day: Soon I'll have another life to care for, whose very survival will rest in my hands.

"I'm floatin' on cloud nine, babe," sings Poppy beside me, her melodic voice now louder than a whisper. The Glossies mimic her, like a cats' chorus, but she seems not to hear—or care—and carries on happily.

"Hope you've got a head for heights, rise up and you'll be mine," I sing, joining in, clicking my fingers to the tinny beat from the iPod. I'm not sure where this burst of defiance has come from. There is a stunned silence from behind us.

"Rise up and you'll be mi-i-ine." Poppy grins at me

as we finish the verse with exaggerated feeling and our eyes screwed up, like the best pop stars.

My phone is vibrating. There's a text from Ed.

Am getting a radio controlled plane. :) As if I'd forgotten!

Race you, I text in reply. My wonderful horse is going to run as swiftly as the wind.

Loser, responds my brother, who by now is probably hitched up to tubes, watching his blood roller-coaster go through its cleaning process.

Suddenly, out of nowhere, I imagine a red jet doing aerobatics, high in the sky. It starts to plummet toward earth. The crowd below holds its breath. Any moment now, its nose will pull out of the dive. Any moment now, applause will ripple across the expectant masses. But the plane is gathering speed and its engines are making a high-pitched scream. In the cockpit, the face behind the visor is ashen, vibrating with the velocity of the fall. I know the features as well as my own, the fine jawbone, the straight nose, the dark pigmented skin on the left cheek. Sweat lines, like silver beads, are strung under his eyes, which are narrowing into slits as the ground looms closer, and beyond it, the ocean.

The pilot is my dad. He is trying to maneuver the plummeting machine toward the expanse of sea. There is a squeal of metal and a jolt and I am fighting to get off the stationary bus. As the doors open, I'm at the front of the surge of bodies that spills out on to the pavement. I stand, face almost pressed into the metal mesh fence, trying to steady my breathing.

I haven't told Mom or Ed about my panic attacks.

"You OK, Jodie?" asks Poppy, her hand lightly on my arm.

"Fine," I nod, managing a smile.

"Thanks for the duet," she adds.

"Maybe we should form a band," I manage to say, before my body is swept along in the tide of Brockenbank students. When I glance back, Poppy's red head is only just above the water.

As I enter my classroom and sit at my desk, I feel my

brow and realize I'm sweating. It's hard to breathe, hard to stop my head from sinking down under the waves.

Slowly, my lungs start to regulate. The ocean morphs into a riot of voices: gossiping, laughing, teasing. Words and faces are becoming distinct. Chairs scrape against the wooden floor as girls and boys assemble for registration.

I'm not drowning this time.

"Jodie?" calls our lovely homeroom teacher.

"Yes, here, Miss Dawson," I reply, grateful to feel the solid floor beneath my feet.

Chapter Six

Warm neck gently steaming. Soft hair hidden by a mane twitching under the pressure from the brush. Mouth nuzzling at my boots. Shod foot idly scraping at the straw in the stable. Tail swishing with pleasure. The sweet, musty smell of hot horse filling the dimly lit space, wafting over the half-closed door and dispersing into the darkening evening. All bad thoughts from the day easing out of my fingertips with every sweep of the brush against flickering flesh.

I put my arm over Rambo's solid shoulder and lean my face against his, staring deep into his left eye, a brown fathomless pool. He raises his front hoof and lets it rest against my left foot.

"Hey you. Leave my boot alone, I know what you're up to," I tell him, as he lets me rub his nose with my fingers. That soft, velvety space between the nostrils is on my top ten list of everything. At this moment, it's probably in my top three, after Mom and Ed (who tie first, natch) and peanut butter M&M's.

He's making faces and showing me his teeth, which are huge and yellow. He's not worried about having a Hollywood smile. I scratch his forelock playfully. He responds by leaning against me and standing on my foot. It's his party trick. I reach into my pocket and produce a piece of browning apple. It's the price for having my foot back.

"You're quite bad," I say, with affection. I've known Rambo for five years, ever since we moved to the Forest after Dad was stationed at Lyntonbury Haven airbase. At first, I wasn't big enough to ride him. It took about eighteen months before I had the strength to handle his habit of grazing on the move. His unsuspecting young riders would often be thrown over his head for the sake of a dandelion or a patch of new grass.

That's never happened to me, though. Rambo and I

have an understanding. He knows that if he's good on a ride, he'll be rewarded with something nice from my pocket.

In his stable, it's a different set of rules. He pushes his luck, but out of fun, not malice. I've lost count of the times I've groomed him, untangled his mane, brushed the mud from his belly, polished his tack, secured his rug, and wished him good night with a kiss between his eyes.

He's not the best-looking horse on the block, but he's been my special responsibility after school and during vacations for so long, he's my number one friend, after Ed. I've waved him off on his rides and welcomed him home with bowls of mash and a one-to-one beauty treatment. I've sat with him when he's been ill and brought him treats on Christmas Day, including my version of carrot cake, a mix of grated carrots and treats, which he loves.

When the world caved in two years ago, and the welfare officer arrived on our doorstep with the worst news ever, I slept with Rambo, curled into the arch of his neck, my tears absorbed into the bristles of his mane. Usually a fidgeter, he didn't move a muscle all night. When dawn broke, he nudged me awake, as if to say, "It's a new day—look." He breathed into my hair, tickling my neck, and even made me smile.

And now, here I am, about to transfer my loyalties to a rival; a phantom horse that still only exists in my imagination, but could soon be taking all my attention.

The thought causes a sharp pain, like a lightning bolt, down my spine. I know this sensation. Guilt. It was a regular visitor after Dad died and I would lie awake wishing I'd done more to make him proud; been kinder, less selfish, a better daughter; spoiled him more on his birthdays, told him I loved him every time he said good night.

"I won't abandon you," I whisper in Rambo's ear. He snorts back at me, softly.

"There. You're perfect and I'm hungry," I tell him, giving him a last scratch on his blaze. I wrap my brush and comb back in my carry roll and shift the stable-door bolt back before Rambo can try his usual delaying tactics—biting my sweater is his favorite. As I secure the lock from the other side, his head appears, his expression full of anticipation.

"Last one, greedy guts," I whisper, delving into my pocket for the final piece of apple. Rambo lifts it from my hand and makes a big deal about chewing it, determined to get every last drop of flavor out of it.

"Night night, Bo," I say, planting a kiss on his head. He yawns, and on his ridiculously long tongue there are bits of squishy apple. "Ugh. Your table manners are awful," I mutter, moving away across the yard, which is quiet, but for the occasional noise of hooves on straw and the contented munching of ponies enjoying their evening feed.

A figure emerges from the side of the office, carrying two pails of water. From her confident stride, I know it's Rachel. She's always the last to leave with Sue, the owner. Sue usually gives her a ride home.

"All done with that bad boy?" she asks me.

"Yup," I reply. Part of me wants to blurt out my good news, yet something is telling me to be cautious. Lots of the girls who come to the stables tell Rachel they are getting their own horse to try and impress her. Often, it's just make-believe. I can't exactly ask her to keep it a secret and I don't want everyone to know just yet. For a while, I want to hold on to it, like a glittering trophy, in the core of my being.

But in good time there will be practical issues to sort out. I'll talk to Sue about boarding and whether I can work some paid hours to offset some of the costs. I'll need tack and equipment and lots of advice about vet checks and health monitoring.

First of all, I must start my search for the finest horse in the land.

"See you tomorrow then," says Rachel cheerfully.

"Okeydokey," I reply brightly. Rachel almost does a double take. She's used to monosyllables from me. *Okeydokey* is out of character; it's Ed's standard phrase and has obviously wormed its way into my subconscious.

Something definitely feels as if it's shifting. As I freewheel out of the yard on my bike and onto the lane, my headlight illuminating the path ahead, the smile on my face is as curvy as the crescent moon.

Chapter Seven

I'm running in my ugly dog pajamas and polar
bear slippers down our drive like a clown, my
bathrobe flapping and its belt dragging on the
path. Charlie Bradstone, who delivers our papers
and is always yabbering into his iPhone, is at this
very moment stuffing the *Times* and the *Hampshire
Clarion* into the green mailbox outside our gate, his
bike between his legs. He looks a bit surprised at my
crazy outfit.

"It was like...well, awesome," he's saying into the
phone. "He was offsides, though, like, totally."

"Morning," I say, climbing the first bar of the
gate, leaning over, and snatching the *Clarion* from the
mouth of the box. Charlie, who is fifteen, stubbly on
odd parts of his face and always half-asleep, raises one

eyebrow (which for him is a gesture of mild shock) as I retreat toward the house.

"Thanks," I call, glancing back over my pastel blue shoulder. Charlie is riding away on his bike, still in conversation. He waves without turning back.

"You shouldn't have done that, Stick," yawns Ed as I slam the front door behind me and wipe my slippers on the mat.

"What?" I ask.

"Terrorized the wildlife," he replies, scampering toward the kitchen, from which fantastic croissant smells are wafting. "The squirrels have died from shock."

"Ha ha," I say, already flicking through the paper to find the small ads at the back.

Mom is up and dressed in jogging pants and a sweatshirt, her hair in a messy pony tail. There's chocolate spread in a jar on the table and some apricot jam we bought from the country fair last month. She's pouring hot, frothy milk into two mugs. She stirs white chocolate flakes into both and gives them to us as we sit down.

"You're up early," I comment as she tweaks my nose.

"Ed wants to go to the plane shop in Southampton," explains Mom.

"That sounds fun, not," I say, pulling a face of mock disgust.

"If you're not shoveling poo, you can come too," suggests Ed, white froth covering his top lip like a mustache.

"It's Saturday, duh." Nothing stops me from going to the stables at the weekend. A pang of something approaching regret grumbles in my stomach. A trip to the city would mean I could check out the ads in all the horsey mags.

My eyes scan the box ads in the *Clarion*—there are several photos of horses, large and small. "Aw, look," I murmur, my gaze drawn to a furry brown dumpling on legs.

"What is it?" asks Mom, removing golden croissants from the oven just as the timer goes off.

"A Shetland named Tubs," I reply.

"Your feet would be on the ground," Ed responds dismissively. "You need one bigger than a toy." For once, he's being sensible.

"How many hands?" I ask, testing him.

"They only have feet, duh."

"So how big's this plane shop?" I say, showing interest.

"Largest in the state," he answers.

"Poor Mom."

"It'll be fun," says Mom, looking on the bright side, as ever.

"It's not like we're going to be in there *all* day," says Ed. "I know what I want."

"I'm all ears," I reply.

"A five-and-a-quarter-foot Spitfire, with hand-painted camouflage color scheme and warbird pilot with removable helmet." Ed beams. "I'm going to get it online, but I want to look at one first."

"You sure you don't need a licence to fly one of those?" I ask.

"Nah. Just a six channel radio and lots of sky," he answers, sending Mom a grateful grin. "Soooo exciting," he mutters, mouth emitting doughy flakes like anti-aircraft fire.

"Gross, little brother," I tell him, shaking my head. He responds by covering his head with a paper napkin.

"Better," I say. Ed pokes eyeholes in the paper so that he can see. He looks like a ghost.

Mom has given each of us a budget of fifteen two thousand dollars for our chosen present and will keep a fund for ongoing costs—travel expenses for finding suitable spots to fly the plane and feed and keep for my horse. My costs will outweigh Ed's by a long shot, so Mom's also putting an equivalent sum in a building society account in Ed's name.

She's being great about everything.

"What about a special treat for you, Mom?" I ask suddenly. It's only just occurred to me that she's left herself out of the equation. She looks a bit taken aback and sad, all at the same time.

"Oh, well. I'll have to think about that, won't I?" she replies thoughtfully.

I feel stupid and insensitive. It's obvious that what she really wants is the one thing she can't have—Dad. Ed makes big eyes at me under his napkin, which tells me I am the dumbest person in the universe. I lower my gaze and return to the "Horses for Sale" columns in the hope there will be something here to spark a new line of conversation.

None of them has the wow factor, though, not even the year-old bay colt with famous grandparents. My heart feels heavy in my chest. I close the paper quietly.

"Nothing?" asks Mom gently, recovering her smile.

"Nope," I reply.

"He, or she, is out there somewhere," she tells me. "Keep your compass open."

"You can't do that, you might stab someone by mistake—that's what they say in math," says Ed.

He's walking around the kitchen, still under his napkin, making a strange humming sound, with a fork and a knife held out in front of him.

"Nutcase," I say, giggling. When I look at Mom, she's chuckling too.

Chapter Eight

I arrive at the stables on my bike just as Rachel is being dropped off by her dad. She's carrying a tray covered in a tea towel, which is good news. Rachel's mom sometimes bakes cakes on the weekend for the team at the stables and it looks like today is our lucky day.

"Hi, Jodie," says Rachel. "Mom's made lemon cupcakes—we're her guinea pigs."

"Wow," I reply, licking my lips and lifting the tea towel to take a peek. The cupcakes smell fantastic. "Actually, there's something I'd like..." I begin, but excited girls have appeared from all corners of the stables and are surrounding Rachel, hoping for a treat.

"Mucking out first, cupcakes later," Rachel laughs, holding the tray out of arm's reach. The girls sigh, disappointed.

I lock my bike to the fence and walk to the office to check on the ride timetable for the day. There's no sign of Sue, but her lists are all set out on the table. I see that Rambo is out twice on hour-long rides. He'll love that, provided his rider is firm and keeps him moving. My initials are next to his name, which means I'm responsible for all aspects of his care, so my first job is to prepare his tack for his nine-thirty ride.

Of all the different areas at the stables, I think I love the tack room the most. Bridles and saddles line the walls, all shapes and sizes, each with a name plate and a photo of a furry face beside them. The low-beamed room smells of leather and linseed oil, saddle soap and horse sweat. It's sweet and musty, warm and inviting. There are spare boots lined up against the wall and lunging reins in one corner. The stone floor always has sawdust on it and the window that overlooks the yard is always steamed up.

Adventures begin here as soon as a bridle is lifted from its hook. The horses sense it even before they hear the clink of metal bits and the scrape of eager boots in the yard. They begin to murmur and whinny, and inquisitive heads appear over stable doors. I know Rambo will already be nibbling his, peeling off a layer of wood with his teeth. He does that when he's excited. I move instinctively to his tack and as I run my hand over his smooth saddle, I feel a familiar thrill run down my spine, even though I'm not riding today.

By the time a group of ten eager riders has arrived in the yard, Rambo is looking his beautiful best; groomed and saddled. I even polished his stirrups with my sleeve. The morning light is making them sparkle. He's nuzzling at my pocket, ever hopeful. I help his rider, a girl of about eleven, mount up and then give him a slice of apple. He snorts his appreciation and is still chewing when Sue appears on Juniper, a chestnut gelding, to lead the line of horses out.

"Walk on," she instructs, and the riders shorten their reins and the sound of forty-four hooves on the move echoes around the yard. I watch Rambo until he's out of sight. He has already tried to eat some low-hanging leaves on a tree. I think Natalie, his rider, might have her hands full for the next hour.

Rachel is organizing the younger helpers, giving them jobs. She's in charge when Sue is out on a ride. She always asks you to do things with a smile and she lets us have the radio on, which is usually against the rules. It keeps everyone happy and makes the work more fun when you can sing along. Misty, one of the Shetlands, even joins in sometimes, but she's tone deaf!

When I look at the clock in the yard, it already reads 10 a.m.

"Cupcake time," says Rachel, a while later, appearing in the open doorway of Rambo's stall.

"Yeah!" I exclaim with a huge grin. I'm always starving by midmorning. I spread the last of the fresh straw on the ground quickly and brush my hands together.

"You do a great job here, Jodie," Rachel tells me, as I pull the bolt across and secure Rambo's door. "Sue really appreciates how hard you work. She thinks you have quite a gift with horses."

"Thanks," I reply proudly. Now's the moment. I take a deep breath. "Actually, there's something I'd like to ask your advice about, both of you."

"Of course, anything," says Rachel.

"I'm getting my own horse," I tell her, quietly, so no one else in the yard hears. My voice has gone quite squeaky because it's so full of excitement.

"Jodie, that's *fantastic*!" she responds, giving me a huge hug. "I'm so happy for you."

"I only just started looking and I wondered if you and Sue could let me know if you hear about any good ones for two thousand dollars?" I ask.

"Of course," agrees Rachel. "Will you want to keep it here?"

"Yes. I need to ask Sue about boarding and whether I can do more hours to help with the costs."

"I'm sure that won't be a problem," confirms Rachel. "I can speak to her first if you like, feel her out."

"Wow," I say. "That would be great, thanks. There's just one thing…"

"You'd like to keep it quiet from the gang," says Rachel, smiling. She reads me like a book. I nod, relieved.

"Just for now, until I get it all together in my head," I tell her.

"That's fine. So let's get those cupcakes handed out. There is enough for everyone. But the others won't know it's a secret celebration," says Rachel, conspiratorially, an arm around my shoulder.

Chapter Nine

It's the first of August and a very special day. That's not just because the weather forecast said it would be the hottest day of the year, or because Ed has gone to his friend Alex's for a sleepover party (his illness usually means he wants to stay at home). Today, Mom and I are going to the New Forest pony sale. More than five hundred horses, ponies, and donkeys are being auctioned. We picked up the advance brochure last week because Sue tipped me off about a lovely pony she'd heard about through the grapevine.

I've waited months to find the right horse. Once the summer vacation started, I agreed with Mom that it would be sensible to buy at the start of vacation, so that my new horse and I could get to know each other really well.

The pony we've come to see is named Lady. She's an eight-year-old chestnut with a good track record in local shows. At fourteen hands, she's going to cope with my ever-lengthening frame. She has a gentle temperament. Her dam was a prize-winning mare called Tiger Lily. In less than five minutes, I will be looking at her in her sale enclosure, and in twelve hours, she might be starting a new life at the stables, with Rambo as her new best friend.

My breathing is short and almost panicky, but from excitement, not fear. I never want Mom to see the attacks that come out of nowhere, narrowing my surroundings into tunnel vision, and causing sweat to pour from my body and nausea to rise from my stomach toward my throat like lava. So far, that doesn't seem to be happening.

Mom is parking and we're getting out into the warm, early morning. The air is full of whinnying—the animals are scared of this clearing in the Forest, with its holding stalls, narrow walkways, and the wooden auction ring. Some must have traveled quite a distance to be here—journeys that began in the dark. They have been tethered for several hours in a moving vehicle, with standing room only. Poor creatures.

We're making our way to the registration vehicle to pick up an auction brochure. This will tell us where Lady is on the order of sale, and once we have her number we can find her in the enclosures. Mom gives our details and pays the fee. We're given a number—four-two-five—on a white card that we can hold up if we're lucky enough to offer the winning bid.

Lady is twentieth on the list and we're pointed in the right direction to go and see her. My palms have gone quite cold, which is spooky. Weird things, which feel like frogs, are leaping about in my abdomen. I want to love her at first sight. But what if we lose her in the bidding? Mom gives me a squeeze. She feels as much on edge as I do.

Suddenly, there's frenzied neighing and whinnying coming from the unloading area—a real commotion with voices raised and the stamping of equine feet on a ramp. The tone coming from this horse is angry, not fearful. I'm intrigued and turn my head to see what's going on.

I'm looking at a gray stallion, ragged and untrimmed, with the most beautiful, arched Arab neck I have ever seen. Two men are trying to lead him with ropes out of the trailer. They're yanking and pulling at the tethers but he is standing firm and proud. He does not want to come out into the crowd that has formed.

I push my way to the front of it, leaving Mom a bit behind. The men are trying to clear a space, waving their arms and tugging at the horse in turn. No wonder he's apprehensive. I feel myself moving forward.

"Stand back!" they warn. Instead, I offer out a hand, indicating that I will take a rope. The men exchange glances, almost smirking. They try to wave me away. The younger man grabs the horse by his forelock and tries to drag him down the ramp. A front hoof lashes out in response.

"He's a devil," says the older man, lifting his cap and wiping his brow. "I'll be glad to get rid of him."

"What's his name?" I ask, holding the horse's backward gaze. The man shoots an irritated look at me.

"Samphire. Like the wild plant. On account of his raggedy mane." He's holding the halter with two hands now, yanking it viciously.

"Hey, Samphire," I say quietly, approaching him, ignoring the man's attempt to block my way. "They need you to come out, boy. Will you walk with me?" I hold my position. Samphire's ears move backward and forward. He extends his nose toward me, sniffs, jerks his head back, stamps his feet. I'm getting the once-over, horse style. His eyes dart between me and the men. He seems to be weighing up his options.

With a deep grumble and a flaring of nostrils, he takes a step forward, then another. The man grudgingly lets me take the halter. I keep it loose and hold eye contact with Samphire. Once down the ramp and on the grass, he raises his head and paws the earth with a hoof.

"He must like you," says the man, taking the halter back from me, a half-smile on his lips. "Never seen him that amenable." He starts to lead Samphire toward the enclosures, but the stallion's feet are sidestepping, resisting his will. "I'll get even with you!" the man shouts, exasperated, as Samphire rears up a little. The stewards are helping now, opening an enclosure door, ushering the animal inside.

Mom has caught up with me. She has a pained and concerned expression, like the one she used to greet me with after I'd run off in a department store and had to be collected from customer service.

"Oh dear." She sighs.

"What?" I ask, half in a dream.

"I know that look," she says. "It means you want that crazy horse."

"I've never wanted anything so much in my life," I answer.

"Don't you think you should look at Lady?" Mom asks. "She's lovely—gentle, quiet, perfect."

"What number is Samphire?" I ask the man, who is leaning on the enclosure door, staring at the horse who is soon to be converted into a fistful of cash.

He takes my auction catalog from my hand, flicks through it and opens up the page where Samphire is listed, pointing to the entry with a black-nailed, mud-stained finger.

"He's there, large as life. Don't you go bidding for him, now. He's not fit for a young'un like you. Someone needs to break his spirit, teach him some manners. He'll probably need a whip, not a whippersnapper, that's my advice."

I read the entry. *Number 50. J. Ingram Esq. Gray Arab cross stallion. 3 Y.O. Moves beautifully. Has been halter broken. Ready to bring on.*

I want to tell him that I don't want his advice and that he's wrong about Samphire. I just know he is. Mom is holding my elbow, urging me to walk away.

With a final glance at the enclosure where Samphire is pacing, ears folded, I let Mom guide me through the crowd, along a walkway, and into the labyrinth of the animal maze. We pass donkeys, miniature Shetlands, Forest ponies, Falabellas—the tiniest of all horses, so tiny you can pick them up and cuddle them. In the holding pens, there's a mixture of singles, doubles, small groups. My head is starting to spin. The air is heavy with dung and straw and fretful snorting.

Moments later, we are right by lot number twenty and I cast my eyes into the space beyond the wooden door, hoping that lightning doesn't strike twice. Lady stands quietly in one corner, chewing hay. Her current owner, a woman in her twenties, is brushing her pony's chestnut coat for a final time before she's taken to the ring. She looks immaculate. Even her hooves are oiled. Her tail is smooth with no hairs twisted. Her mane is cropped and combed and she has recently been clipped too.

"There," says Mom encouragingly. "Isn't she gorgeous?"

"She's a bit like a horse the Glossies would ride, all pretty and perfect." This comes out of my mouth like a big criticism and her owner, who happens to be wearing pink lipstick, gives me a withering look. I know that if I hadn't seen Samphire, I would probably have fallen for Lady. But even now, I can hear his whinny above all the others. It's as if he's speaking to me, as if we've connected somehow.

I'm starting to feel quite sick. I hate it when Mom disapproves of things I'm thinking or doing. And I'm about to do something so reckless it might cause real trouble between us, which would be unbearable.

But something is telling me Samphire and I should be together. It's not logical to want a crazy horse. But this isn't about logic. It's a feeling coming from somewhere so deep inside, a place I thought was buried away, never to be pried open. I don't have control over it, now that it's escaped. It seems to be controlling me.

"We should go find a seat in the arena," says Mom, her voice a little hushed to mask her frustration.

We leave Lady and work our way to the circular, wooden structure. Inside, the seats are raked and there's a small, round space at the center. A raised, enclosed box with glassless windows gives the auctioneer a roof over his head. He's sitting waiting, tapping his microphone every so often to make sure the sound system is working.

We find two spaces on the wooden trestle benches and sit down. Mom studies the catalog, trying to avoid confrontation with me. I think she hopes she'll find a last-minute alternative to the horse of my dreams, which is the horse of her nightmares.

"He's not even properly broken in, Jodie," Mom says at last. "He's not used to being ridden."

"Maybe he's just been with the wrong people," I reply. I know Mom's right. By the age of three, he should be rideable.

"What if he's too wild to tame?" she asks. "He's a stallion, after all."

"I'll find that guy who whispers in horses' ears," I

reply with a shrug.

"I think Dad would be saying no," counters Mom. That was a bit below the belt.

"I bet Granny and Granddad didn't want him to fly jets, but he made up his mind and he knew the risks," I respond. My eyes are pricking. I'm *so* not going to cry.

Mom sighs. And then she smiles, pushing some hair off her face. "That's just the kind of thing he would have said," she comments. "I could never win an argument against him. But you know the budget, Jode. Two thousand tops because of the tax on top. If it goes above that, you have to let him go."

"Okeydokey," I confirm, swallowing hard.

There are now no seats anywhere. Looking around, it's a sea of T-shirts; mutts on leashes; families; individuals; owners; dealers. There's noise from the many excited conversations, heads bowed over the catalogs, pens circling chosen animals.

Moments later, the wooden gate leading to the enclosures swings open and a frightened foal of about six months is ushered into the arena. It runs around the perimeter, trying to avoid the female usher who is tasked with keeping it on the move so that buyers can assess its condition.

"Good morning, ladies and gentleman," says the auctioneer from his raised booth. "Welcome to the New Forest sale for August. Can I remind you that the currency for sale of the lots is in dollars today. Bidders must be registered and have a card. Please do not bid unless you have this card, otherwise your bid will be void. Thank you all. Let's get down to business. First up today, we have this bay filly foal, bred in the Forest. Sire is Mr. Brumby. Dam is Magic Flute. A nice example. Can we say ten dollars? Twelve dollars, fourteen dollars..."

Bidding gets off to a flying start. The auctioneer's voice becomes a chant of figures, rhythmic, compelling. I'm trying to follow the action in the crowd and see who's raising their hand or nodding to raise the stakes. It all happens so fast, yet the auctioneer's eyes miss nothing.

"Thirty-one dollars, are we all done at thirty-one dollars? Going once, going twice, all done now, sold to the lady on my left. Raise your number, please. Thank you."

The woman, who seems to be alone, looks very pleased. Her foal is being herded out of the arena through a different door into a narrow corridor, which leads back to the enclosures. A new pony is entering now. The process seems very smooth and well organized. In less than three minutes, the foal has changed ownership and is starting a new life. I hope she will be happy.

Bidding for the pony gets underway and once again is brisk and determined. This time, an elderly man raises his pipe to increase his offers. The pony is his for thirty-five dollars. It seems such a small amount of money. You can't buy a dog for that.

Looking down into the arena, it reminds me of that film where the Roman gladiators fight with lions as entertainment for the crowds. At least here the animals are unhurt and their ordeal in the ring only lasts a few minutes.

Very soon, it is Lady who is brought in. Her owner, the woman with the pink lipstick, runs athletically by her side as she trots round the perimeter, head high, feet lifted and sure.

"And here we have a fine example of a filly from the Mansbridge family stable. Jenny Mansbridge showing her today. Both, if I might say, very well turned out."

There is laughter from the crowd and a nod in thanks from Jenny. It seems that many of the owners are known to the buyers. The world of horses is quite close-knit. The friendship is always competitive, though, even at my stables.

Mom is clasping her hands together. "I think you could be making a big mistake," she warns. "That horse is perfection on legs. She wouldn't hurt you."

"Samphire won't hurt me," I tell her, holding her gaze. "I know he won't."

"Do we have one hundred and fifty dollars? Two hundred, two hundred and fifty..." The auctioneer's voice buzzes in my head, a monotone drone, that becomes like a drill hammering into the recesses of my brain.

For an awful moment, I think Mom is going to bid for Lady. She raises her hand and the auctioneer's steely gaze alights on her, his eyebrows raised.

"Mom!"

"Sorry," she mouths and his attention moves away swiftly, scanning the crowd. "I was just trying to ease my shoulder," she explains. Mom's had a slightly frozen shoulder since Dad died. It's as if part of her locked up that day.

"Four hundred and eighty, five hundred. Five hundred and fifty..."

The bidding is animated. Lady is standing center stage, snorting prettily. She knows her worth, right down to her dainty fetlocks.

"Six hundred and fifty dollars, seventy. Seven

hundred dollars and fifty from my right. Eight hundred, thank you, sir. Nine hundred. One thousand on my left. Eleven twelve, thirteen hundred. Are we all done at thirteen hundred for this lovely filly? Thirteen hundred once, twice, and all done, thank you, the lady in the central aisle."

The wooden gavel hits the block and Lady's fate is sealed. I lean forward to get a good look at the woman who has bought her. A girl a little younger than me is jumping up and down next to her, waving her arms in the air. Her smile is as wide as a crescent moon. I can appreciate the surge of joy she must be feeling. I hope that, soon, I will be in the same position.

As Lady leaves the ring, Jenny kisses her on the head. It's strange how some animals have charmed lives, full of affection, and others have years of misery and cruelty. It's often just down to how they look and where they're born. It's the same for people too, I suppose. The luck of the draw, as Dad would have said.

We're on lot number thirty-eight now. There are

only five more until the moment of truth, as two of the lots consist of several animals.

My legs are numb from the wooden bench and I'm digging my heels into the planks beneath my sneakers. We may well go home without a horse today, if the bidding doesn't go my way, and for the rest of my life I will remember the moment Samphire was nearly mine.

Mom takes my hand and grips it as lot number forty-nine, a miniature Shetland, is sold for two hundred and twenty dollars. Its small frame scurries through the exit door in a flurry of hooves and tail tossing.

There is a sudden hush throughout the crowd. Lot number fifty has not yet appeared. There is the sound of shod feet lashing out against wood and men's voices and then an angry whinny rises above all the others from the enclosures.

Samphire. He is not going to come quietly.

The wooden gate into the arena crashes back and the horse that canters in, halter lead dangling, causes voices to exclaim all around me in a wave of surprise and interest.

Samphire enters alone. The man stays well back behind the gate, shaking his head, rubbing his leg, which has probably just suffered a well-placed kick.

My heart is banging like a hammer on a trash can lid. It seems even the crowd noise is drowned out now. I'm looking at Samphire, who is trotting, wheeling, rearing when he gets too near the faces in the front row. People are whispering, wondering who will dare take on this wild creature.

Mom's grip is hurting my hand. I shake it free. I need all my limbs for what is to come, all my concentration.

"Ready?" Mom asks. I nod, noticing that the color has drained from her face. Maybe it's just that my eyes are seeing everything in black and white. Oh please no! I know what comes next. I don't want this to happen. Not the tunnels, not the sickness and the fainting. Not now, of all times! I have to see this through. I have to try.

"Lot number fifty. A spirited, part-Arab three-year-old stallion from Mr. Ingram, halter broken. Shall we begin at one hundred and fifty dollars."

The auctioneer is beginning his patter. I try to lengthen my breathing. My palms are wet with cold sweat. I raise one hand with as much strength as I can muster.

"One hundred and fifty dollars, we have one hundred and seventy, two hundred..."

My head is spinning. *Jodie, get a grip!* My hand is going up and down like a signal at a railroad crossing. Mom is holding her breath, staring at her clasped hands.

"Two hundred dollars, two fifty, three hundred..."

The bidding is ferocious. We're at a thousand, then fifteen hundred, in a matter of seconds. When we reach the nineteen hundred dollars marker, I am shaking from head to foot, holding my gaze on the auctioneer, doing my best not to see the agitated, ragged creature trying to find an escape route just below me. If he could grow wings, like Pegasus in the myth, he would fly—I just know he would.

"Nineteen hundred and twenty, nineteen hundred and fifty on my right, are we going on? Yes, we are."

I'm raising my hand for a bid of two thousand, knowing that this is it, it's as far as I can go. There are tears welling in the corners of my eyes now.

"Two thousand we have, are we done at two thousand?"

Please let it be done, please let it be done.

"Two thousand once, twice, and oh, two thousand and fifty from a latecomer on my right."

I gasp as the pent-up emotion finally escapes and my body crumples against Mom's, which is rigid as if made of stone. I have closed my eyes. I don't want to see the person who has just ended my dreams. I don't want their face to be etched in my memory forever.

"Two thousand and fifty dollars now. Are we done, ladies and gentlemen? I see two thousand...one hundred. Two thousand one hundred we have. Are we concluded? Going once, at two thousand one hundred. Going twice, all done for this stallion at two thousand one hundred."

The gavel comes down with a bang that sends a shudder from my teeth to my toes.

"Can you raise your card please?" asks the auctioneer.

I feel Mom shift in her seat. She must be easing her shoulder again. Her left arm is wrapped around me protectively. I glance at her face, which is set and determined. Just beyond it, I see something white, elevated.

"Oh, Mom!" I can barely speak.

"He's yours, Jodie. That horse needs a second chance," is all she says. We're both fighting back tears.

"Thank you," I say, before everything goes black.

Chapter Ten

When I come to, my head is between my knees and I'm in some sort of a tent that smells like medicine. A woman in blue is rubbing my cold hands. Mom is next to me, kneeling on the matting, which covers the bare earth. I recognize her shoes.

"Hi," I say. My head is throbbing. I sit up slowly and let my vision settle.

"That was quite a reaction," says Mom, feeling my forehead. Memories rush back into my empty brain. A smile spreads across my face as my mind catches up. The closest thing to ecstasy I have ever experienced travels from my stomach to my heart, which suddenly aches with pleasure.

"Wow," I say. "I've got a horse!"

"That's nice, dear," says the woman rubbing my

hands. I look at her more closely. She has gray hair and a name tag that says "Nurse" on it. "Would you like some water?"

"Yes, please," I answer. She stands and pours some from a jug on a nearby table into a paper cup, giving it to me. I sip and it tastes like ice.

"Have you fainted before?" she asks. Now isn't the time to 'fess up, I'm thinking. I don't want Mom to be extra worried about me.

"Nope," I lie. I've managed to conceal my problem from everyone so far. I know if the school finds out that I've passed out in the restrooms a couple of times after my panic attacks, Mom will be called in for a chat and they'll all start keeping a special eye on me.

"That's good. I'm going to take your blood pressure, just to make sure. I'll just wrap this pad around the top of your arm, dear," she says. I think she's the oldest nurse I've ever seen. From the look of her wrinkles, she must be at least a hundred.

Suck, suck, suck, goes the wrapper on my arm,

getting tighter and tighter, as she pumps the black rubber sphere attached to a tube. She checks the numbers on the dial. *Sssssss* goes the air as it is released. Now she's feeling my pulse in my right wrist and looking at the watch on her uniform.

"That's all fine," the nurse confirms with a smile. I notice that her teeth are very small and neat. She unwraps the pressure pad from my arm and tidies the equipment away.

Mom still looks concerned. "Are you sure she's all right?" she asks the nurse.

The woman smiles. "Right as rain, I'd say. Just the heat and excitement getting the better of her."

"Great," says Mom. "Do you feel ready to walk, Jodie? If not, I'll leave you here and sort out the payment and paperwork for change of ownership. We need to call Sue too, so that she can bring the trailer."

"I'm good," I confirm, standing up to prove it. My legs feel a bit spongy, but otherwise, everything is back to normal. "Thank you," I say to the nurse.

"You're welcome, dear," she replies. "I hope you enjoy your new horse."

"I will," I answer with certainty.

"Let's just go and see him before we tackle the paperwork," says Mom, reading my mind. She slips an arm around my waist and we walk toward the enclosures. There are fewer people around now as the auction is still going on. It's easy to find our way to Samphire's stall.

"Hey, you," I say to the noble gray head, which is sticking out over the door. "You could use a bath," I tell him, noticing the clumps of dried mud matted into his mane. "Bet you don't like being washed, though."

I take a photo of him on my phone and send it to Ed, followed by a text: *Guess who's sleeping in your bed tonight?*

I let Samphire sniff me for several minutes before I try to touch him. His nostrils flare and push at my clothes, my neck, my hair, my face. He makes a strange sound every so often, a cross between a small whinny and a cough. After a while, he lets his head rest near mine, just a few inches away. He watches me with his left eye.

I move my hand slowly to his neck and run it down toward his chest with a gentle pressure. His back foot stamps and his head shakes. His eye doesn't leave my face, though. He allows me to repeat the movement. This time, there's no agitation, just a flickering across his skin, the muscles responding to my touch. His body is taut, though, braced for combat or escape.

"Friends?" I ask him. He turns his face toward me and flicks his ears back and forth. Without thinking, I scratch the temple between them, just as I do with Rambo, who loves that kind of spoiling. Samphire's head jerks back. His eyes are suddenly white and fearful. He backs into the corner of the stall, kicking out at the partition, tossing his straggly mane and snorting.

I'm looking him square in the face, trying to show him I'm not like the other people who have mistreated him. He can trust me. But the huge challenge ahead is beginning to become clear. I hope I'm up to it. I never want to let Samphire down.

Mom puts her hand on my shoulder. She's reading my mind again. Her touch is strong, reassuring. It tells me that we're in this together.

"The best friendships take time to grow," she says. "And then they last a lifetime."

Chapter Eleven

My phone is buzzing and vibrating. It's a text from Ed:
OMG u bought Shadowfax. Gandalf will b mad. Has been looking everywhere 4 him.

Samphire not Shadowfax. Part Arab. Still want to race? I reply. I think Samphire will beat his plane any day. If Samphire lets me on his back, that is.

Need to go to pilot course first. Says not for beginners on box, comes the response.

So does mine, I text back.

I'm sitting in the front of the Land Rover with Sue and we're pulling into the yard with Samphire in the trailer behind us. There's quite a crowd waiting, including Rachel, the girls who help out on Saturdays, and some parents. Mom has beaten us to it and is sitting on a hay bale outside the office.

It's always an event, a new arrival at Whitehawk Farm Stables. Today, even the horses in the yard sense something is going on and are snuffling at their tethers.

In moments, I'm out of the Land Rover and unlatching the back of the trailer. Sue helps me lower it. I enter with caution, letting Samphire know that I'm coming, resting my hand on his rump, then his shoulder, finally untying his rope. Somehow, I have to back him out of this crate and I already know what he thinks of this kind of transport.

"Off you go," I tell him, giving his chest a gentle push. No reaction, just a flaring of nostrils and a stamping of feet. "You're home now."

This is a horse that needs incentives. I produce a carrot from my pocket and let him sniff it. His lips attempt to smother and snatch it away. I throw it to Sue, who gives Samphire a whistle. He makes a disgruntled rumbling sound, drops his head, paws the floor of the trailer, and starts to move backward.

Once outside, Sue gives him the carrot, which he

munches hungrily, and everyone gathers around to take a closer look. Mom has instructed them not to touch him for now, as he's nervous and unpredictable.

"He's a beauty, Jodie," says Rachel. "What's his name?"

"Samphire," I reply proudly. "He needs breaking in. Hope your offer to help is still open," I add with a grin.

"You bet," replies Rachel, pleased.

After answering lots of questions from the other girls about where he came from and how we nearly lost him at the auction, I walk him to the back of the yard and tether him to a ring so that I can give him a good groom. It also means he's out of the way of the returning three o'clock ride. Mom joins me and gives me a sandwich she bought at a garage on the way back from the auction. I hadn't realized how hungry I was until now.

"I'll be off, then," she says, giving me a hug. "See you later." We've planned a girls' night in, with face masks and nail polish.

"This is the best day of my life, thanks to you," I tell her. Mom looks quite emotional and puts her hand on Samphire's neck. He quivers under her touch, unsure.

"I think he's a great addition to our family," she says. I'm thinking that's not quite how she really feels, but I'm sure she'll love him too, in time.

"Here, give him this," I suggest, handing Mom another carrot from my pocket. I show her how to keep it flat on her hand so that his mouth can take it easily. Samphire buttons his lips and turns his head away. Mom shrugs, disappointed, and hands the treat back to me. She's not really a horsey person, but she's trying hard, for my sake.

Samphire is sniffing the air, trying to work out where he is. His neck is arched and he flicks his tail, even though there are no flies.

Mom walks away down the yard, her easy stride making her hair swing from right to left. There's a spring in her step that I haven't noticed before. Her new job is already bringing changes for us all. I feel so lucky. I know Ed does too. Mom is always thinking about us and trying to make our lives full and happy. As happy as they can be without Dad.

If there was a school for moms, she would definitely be one of the best students.

Samphire is stamping his front right foot now, letting me know he's agitated. Cautiously, I lift it to check his shoe and see that the metal is worn and slightly loose. After skittering left and right, he lets me look at the other three in turn. They are in a similar condition.

"That's the first job, then. New shoes," I say, making a mental note to speak to Sue and arrange for the farrier to visit Samphire when he next comes to the stables. It feels good, and grown-up, to be making these decisions, like I've entered a new world. I'm not a kid anymore. I have real responsibilities in the shape of one big, beautiful, crazy horse.

Chapter Twelve

"Whoaaaah!" says Ed, almost toppling off his bike. "It's really hard pedaling backward."

"Well, get off and walk then," I tell him.

"Nah," responds Ed. "S'OK. I'm good."

Samphire doesn't agree. He finds Ed's antics quite alarming and is sidestepping down the lane. I thought a gentle walk to break in his new shoes would be a great idea, but I didn't expect two-wheeled company. It was a surprise that Ed got up early to come with us, but I'm glad he wants to get to know Samphire.

"And now, it's Edward J. Palmer, going for the world record..." Ed yells, taking off down the lane at top speed and disappearing around a corner. Samphire stops dead in his tracks and snorts loudly, flaring his nostrils.

"I know, he's a pain, but you'll get used to him," I tell my nervous horse. "Walk on." It's been two weeks since the auction but my new, wonderful horse hasn't calmed down.

Samphire's feet are planted firmly on the tarmac. It takes me about five minutes and a bribe involving peppermints to persuade him to move forward. When we reach the bend, Ed's bike is lying on the verge by a gate, but Ed is nowhere to be seen.

"Ed!" I call.

"Over here, Stick," he replies from a distance. He's waving from the cabin of a tractor, halfway across a field. There's no sign of the driver. Ed is bouncing up and down on the seat, pretending to drive. I motion for him to get out.

"It's a John Deere 8120," he shouts as he jumps down and runs toward me. "Two-hundred horse power. Imagine two hundred Samphires pulling at once."

"Amazing, Teddy." I actually can't imagine that. I'm having trouble coping with just one Samphire.

He's decided he would rather be on the other side of the lane, as far away from my brother as possible. "Listen," I say to Ed, "why don't you ride on to the start of the bridle path and we'll meet you there? I'll time you, if you like. Shout when you get there."

This does the trick. Ed loves a challenge.

"Okeydokey," he calls, picking up his bike. He makes revving and screeching noises and swerves away, his front tire in the air. Samphire whinnies and rears up.

"There's no need to copy him," I say, using all my strength to steady the frightened animal. My left arm is in the air and Samphire continues to shy away, flinging his head left and right. It's a battle to bring him down again. He wheels around, knocking me off my feet and, before I know it, I'm rolling down a small slope at the side of the road and into a ditch. The squelch that follows tells me I've landed in something less than good. My nose confirms that I'm lying in stagnant mud, which stinks. Ugh!

Luckily, Samphire isn't running off. He's looking at me, making a nickering noise. I ease myself up and back up the bank. My left side, my hands, and my face are brown and filthy. I take Samphire's halter rein gently. He's standing quietly now, a model horse. I find a lump of carrot in my pocket and offer it to him. He sniffs it, looks away, sniffs it again. We stand, staring at one another for at least a minute. He's testing me, trying to work out if the treat is a trick. Eventually, his long tongue sweeps over my hand and he munches noisily. His pushes a hopeful nose toward me and snuffles my jacket.

"I'm sorry about that, boy," I say to him. "Did they beat you, your last owners?" I will always take care not to raise my arms quickly ever again. I stroke his nose, very gently. He makes a strange, grumbling grunt and paces backward.

"No, you don't. Come here, Samphire." I keep my voice very calm and the rein loose in my hand. I try to relax my body so I don't show him any tension. "That's it, good boy," I encourage, as he takes his first step toward me. "That wasn't so bad, was it?"

I start to lead him forward, and this time, he moves with long, easy strides. I increase my speed to a comfortable jog. Samphire is trotting now, the steels on his hooves clattering on the lane. It feels like a first; we're moving together. He has such an elegant way of lifting his legs and holding his neck. I feel proud, exhilarated, and relieved all at the same time. We're making progress, slowly but surely. His last owner was so wrong about him. He's not a devil horse, just a damaged one who needs time to heal.

"Hahahahah!" laughs Ed, as Samphire and I reach the beginning of the horse trail. "Actually, it's an improvement—brown suits you."

"Yeah, very funny," I sigh.

"Aaargh, you really stink," he yells, holding his nose. "So, what was my time?" he asks.

"I didn't hear you shout," I tell him.

"Aw, Stick, I yelled three times." Ed kicks at the ground with his sneaker. He picks up a twig and draws a line on the ground.

"Sorry, Teddy," I tell him. I want to hug him, but he holds a hand up to stop me from crossing the line. "Will this help?" I produce a chocolate wafer in a wrapper and throw it to him.

"Oh yeah, oh yeah!" he declares, doing a funny dance, then unwrapping the treat and stuffing it into his mouth. Samphire whinnies. It sounds like a protest.

"Oh, OK, here's yours," I say, finding the other carrot and offering it to him. Ed and Samphire exchange glances, each chomping greedily. Ed gives him the thumbs up. Samphire snorts and shakes his mane. I think they've become friends.

It must be a boy thing.

Chapter Thirteen

The moment of truth. After more than three weeks of halter-walking Samphire, getting him used to his surroundings, his new stablemates, and the feel of unfamiliar tack against his skin, I'm going to mount him today. Sue thinks he's been used to riders since there's a girth strap imprint in his belly hair. She says he may have had a bad experience—an accident, even—and that's why he was labeled "unbroken" by his previous owner.

I want to tell him I understand about scars caused by pain and sadness, scars that can't be seen. I know I have to earn his trust. But I must also prove to him that I'm not a pushover who will tolerate bad behavior. If he has no respect for me, we'll never make progress. I think he knows I'm nervous about today—he can sense it.

We're in the yard. Sue and Rachel are with me. Rachel is riding Rambo and Sue is going to teach us in the outdoor ring, if we get that far.

Samphire is sidestepping and arching his neck as I shorten the reins. When my foot slips into the left stirrup, he wheels around, knocking me to the ground. Sue helps me up. I feel embarrassed and a bit taken aback. I look at Rambo with sudden pangs of nostalgia.

"Let's walk him up there," suggests Sue. "Follow Rambo—he'll get the idea."

I take his reins and fall in step behind my old favorite, who clip-clops up the ramp by the side of the office toward the training circle. Samphire keeps pace with me, his head by my shoulder. I don't look at him. He needs to know he's in my bad books.

The ring is enclosed by fencing in a small field. We enter by the gate and wait for Sue to take up her position in the center of a circle worn to dirt by the pounding of hooves. I've had an occasional lesson in here before, when I've earned enough time through helping out. It feels strange to be back again in these new circumstances. After what just happened, my confidence is quite shaken.

"Ready to try again?" asks Sue gently. I nod and take Samphire's reins in my left hand, holding the stirrup with my right. "As lightly as you can," she advises.

I give a little spring and am halfway toward the saddle, but Samphire is skittering away sideways. I'm holding on to the pommel as hard as I can and not letting go and when he reaches the fencing and can go no farther, I swing my leg over and sit firmly on his back.

"Well done, Jodie!" calls Sue. "Try and rein him in now. Nothing sharp. Keep your movements firm and determined, show him who's boss."

He is, I'm thinking, as Samphire takes me on a fast trot around the field, as close to the wooden posts as he dares. Any moment now, he'll scrape me off and make a run for it. He *is* a devil horse, after all. I've worked twenty hours this week to pay for his food and stabling and this is how he repays me.

"I'll put the lunge rein on and see what happens," says Sue, approaching. Rambo is watching all this patiently, occasionally snorting into the warm afternoon air.

Samphire's having none of it. He's pressing me against the gate and I'm raising my right leg at forty-five degrees to avoid it being totally squashed.

"I have an idea," says Rachel. "What if Jodie rides Rambo and shows Samphire what to do?"

"It's worth a try," agrees Sue, dropping the lunge rein on the ground. As she does so, my hyper animal seems to calm down. He lowers his head and breathes heavily, allowing me to pull my leg back. I dismount quickly, my head hot with frustration. My hair is clinging to my forehead under my hat.

"Just walk away," says Sue. "Don't look at him. Go straight to Rambo."

Rachel has dismounted and gives me the reins. I swing up on to Rambo's sturdy back, adjust the stirrups, and encourage my old friend into a lively walk, circling Sue. On her command, we trot and then ease into a controlled canter. Samphire watches, pawing the grass, his ears forward and his gaze never leaving us.

"He's jealous," Sue calls to Rachel, who's gone to sit on the fence. She nods and smiles.

After ten minutes of perfect lessons, shortening and lengthening strides, turning, maneuvering, Rambo and I take a rest. I lean forward and give him a carrot from my pocket. Sue approaches and pats his neck fondly.

"What should I do now?" I ask her. I'm still not making eye contact with the gray barbarian.

"Let Rachel take Rambo back to the yard. We'll see what Samphire's like when there's no competition," she replies. I think she would make a great horse psychologist.

"I hope you're free tonight, because I think you need pizza," says Rachel, approaching.

"Yes, please!" I reply, my spirits lifting suddenly. Rachel knows just what to do to improve a bad situation.

A few seconds later, we're alone, Sue, Samphire, and I. It's like one of those Westerns, when everyone is braced, ready to go for their gun. Samphire is looking at Sue and me and making the strange grumbling noise through his nostrils.

"Should I call him?" I ask. If I go to him, it's telling him he's won. Sue nods. I make my usual clicking sound, which signals I want him to approach. Nothing. I feel in my pocket for treats. They're all gone. This is getting stupid.

Then something really odd happens. Samphire starts to whinny and paw the ground at the same time. The piercing noise travels up and down in pitch, punctuated with snorts and shaking of his head.

"He's talking to you," says Sue, astonished. "I think he's explaining why he's been such a pain."

"It's his song," I tell her. "He's done it before, a little bit. Nothing like this, though."

"He's really getting something off his chest," Sue says. "I think it's best if I leave you two to it. Don't push things. He may have done enough for today."

She turns and moves purposefully out of the ring, through the gate, and out of sight. I know she's just a shout away if I need her, which is reassuring. Samphire stops his noise and just breathes and snorts, swishing his tail.

"That was quite a performance. Will you come now?" I ask tentatively, holding my palm toward him. I hold my breath as he lifts his left hoof, lets it dangle a moment, then places it down nearer to me. The right follows. He stretches his beautiful neck and sniffs the air around me.

"All the way." Three strides later, his face is just in front of mine. He mouths his bit awkwardly, trying to spit it out. Suddenly, I feel guilty. It's probably been a long time since he's had to deal with metal in his mouth. It probably feels awful—something so hard champing at the soft flesh.

"Good boy," I tell him, meaning it. "We're going to try this one more time. OK?"

I prepare the reins and find the stirrup. If he runs amok this time, I'll have to call Sue back. My body is tense from exertion. I mentally count to three and swing myself up and onto the saddle. Samphire grunts and starts to move backward very fast. This is an almost impossible feat for a horse—any dressage rider would think it was very clever. I don't have time to find the other stirrup before he has pushed his backside into the fencing.

Nice one, Samphire. Now you're going to rear up and dump me over into the field.

Surprisingly, this isn't what happens next. When I urge him with my calves against his belly, he starts to walk forward and when I draw my right rein in, he turns elegantly. He's responding to my commands and marking a circle and I want to shout with joy, but that would be ridiculous. We can't both behave like divas. And there's no audience.

It's just me and him—and maybe that's how he wanted it. I'll always remember this as the special day he chose to tell me his story and let me hear all of his song. I would give anything to understand it.

Chapter Fourteen

I'm home, showered, dressed, made-up, and ready to go in about half an hour flat. My bruised pride and aching muscles are fading from my mind. I was so proud of Samphire at the end of the training session, I can forgive him for anything.

Ed threw a mock tantrum when I told him I was going out for pizza without him. "Don't worry about us, Stick," he'd said, leaning against Mom. "The favorite child will stay behind and take care of our mom."

He's such an idiot sometimes.

But secretly, I knew he was pleased that he and Mom are having an evening together. He has already got a stack of DVDs and snacks ready. As a special treat, he's requested fish sticks, mashed potatoes, peas, and cheese sauce for dinner. To each their own.

There's a honk from the lane. Rachel's arrived. Her dad is dropping us off in town and picking is up later, our very own chauffeur. I'm running downstairs two at a time, not easy in ankle boots with heels. I glance in the full-length mirror on the wall in the hall as I pass. My jeans and cropped jacket are an improvement on my usual mucking-out clothes, I'm thinking. Mom and Ed are waiting by the front door.

"You look very nice, darling," says Mom. She's staring quite hard at my mascara, though.

"You look very nice, darling," echoes Ed, air-kissing me.

"Have a lovely time," adds Mom.

"Don't come back too early," says Ed, shooing me out of the door.

"Charming," I say, messing up his hair as I leave.

Rachel has gotten out of the car and gives me a hug. She's wearing jeans and a long leather jacket. Her hair is down and almost reaches her waist. She looks totally different out of her stable clothes too.

"Hi," she says excitedly. "You look great. And I hope you're hungry," she adds. "I'm starving."

"Hi, Mr. Holmes," I say to Rachel's dad as I get into the back seat. "Thanks for picking me up."

"Hello, Jodie," he replies. "You can call me Mark, you know. Rachel has been telling me that you're a horse whisperer."

"Oh, not really." I'm trying not to blush. "I bought a horse at auction—he's a bit of a handful. Rachel's been amazing, helping me with his training. I rode him today for the first time."

"That must have been great," says Mark. He's looking at me in his rearview mirror. I nod and smile.

"It felt a bit like climbing Everest," I tell him after thinking about it for a moment.

"Samphire has a real bond with Jodie. It's amazing, after the state he was in," says Rachel.

"Do you ride?" I ask her dad. He and Rachel exchange glances. She pulls a face at me.

"He sat on a horse once," she says. "Facing the

103

wrong way."

"I prefer things with engines that do as they're told," Mark laughs.

The drive into town takes about ten minutes. I'm sorry when it's over—the three of us have been chatting and laughing the whole time. Mark drops Rachel and me outside Mama Lemon's pizza restaurant, honks, and waves good-bye.

"He's really nice, your dad," I tell Rachel.

"Yeah, although Mom doesn't always agree when he's making loads of noise in the garage. He's got this thing for old cars." Rachel is looking at the menu behind the glass. "Mmmm, smell those pizzas," she says, taking my arm. "Make sure you leave room for the chocolate brownies, Jode. They're as big as the plates, no kidding." She demonstrates with her hands.

"Thanks for everything today," I tell her as we open the door.

"I really admire what you're doing," she replies unexpectedly. "You should be proud of yourself.

Samphire's a big challenge, but he's going to be incredible by the time you're finished with him."

"I hope so," I say.

"I know so," Rachel states. "Now, it's my treat, remember, so you can have anything you want. It's not every day you climb Everest."

Chapter Fifteen

I'm flying, following the curve of the hill, the
September wind blowing with full force into my face.
I lean farther into it, feeling tears on my cheeks and
autumn air rushing to the back of my throat when
I breathe. I am curled, aerodynamic, focused on the
landscape around me. To my left, acres of red-orange
bracken and spindly shrubs, as far as the eye can see.
To my right, tall conifers, standing to attention in
carefully tended rows. Ahead, a path leading toward
mighty oaks and majestic beech trees, the gatekeepers
to the wild woods.

Beneath me, my amazing Samphire, galloping
with a fleetness of foot through this ancient forest. He
follows the path instinctively, his hooves pounding
softly into moss and leaf mulch. I feel electric with his

energy—glowing. From a distance, we are probably a luminous, moving beacon; a UFO.

We pass a pair of ponies grazing. We startle a muddy pig, rooting among the ferns.

"Hello, Mr. Pig!" I call to him.

He grunts irritably and scuffles away over toadstools with colorful heads like upturned tea saucers.

Samphire and I leave the open ground, with its amber foliage, and enter the woods, which are streaked with bright shafts of sun. There's mist between the trees. Water droplets plop from the branch of a dead beech tree, standing silver-gray and ghostly, shocked by the lightning bolt that sapped its life in a second.

Deeper and deeper, we move into the Forest. Samphire's hooves are thudding into mud; his pace slows to a careful canter. He needs no encouragement to continue. He senses there is a destination.

I sometimes dream about the place we're coming to, the secret space Dad and I discovered two years ago, just before he died. It was the result of one of his famous "short cuts," which took us miles out of our circular ride. It's sacred to me now. And bringing Samphire here is an initiation, perhaps for us both. I feel driven to do it. I don't know what to expect—the spirit of Dad to be waiting? A glimpse of the fairies with owl faces who live in the woods? (Nice one, Dad!)

The light ahead is almost dazzling. We're almost there. The trees give way to a clearing about the size of a large paddock, with banks sloping down to a lake as still as a mirror. Samphire slows to a stop and steam from his coat starts to mingle with the mist around us. When I look at the water, there's a reflection of us staring back.

It feels like I'm looking at the present and into the future, to all the fantastic days ahead with this beautiful horse. I see no trace of sadness in our watery images, no ripples of the past.

"They're behind us now, boy, those bad times," I say as I dismount and loop the reins over Samphire's head. I can see a level spot where he can drink. We walk by the lake's edge, accompanied by a frog hopping from leaf to leaf among the foliage. A fallen tree trunk lies by the water. Samphire arches his neck over it and sniffs the unknown substance on the other side. His nostrils blow several times before he drinks. I sit astride the tree, remembering.

A shiver passes up my spine. There's a rustle to our right, a startled face, then the gleam of a brown coat in sunlight, darting away in swift leaps.

"It's just a deer, Sam," I tell him. "Nothing to be afraid of."

He lets me rest my head against his neck. I'm already excited at the prospect of the ride home and I feel he is too. I love every minute I spend with him. Riding him, rubbing him down, putting his coat on, and feeding him have become the highlights of my day.

I smile when I think of Ed's enthusiasm for tractors, planes, and all things mechanical. We're so different in that way.

Light is shafting into the clearing, turning the lake

liquid silver. Dad said this was a magical place and he's right. It takes my breath away.

"I'm so glad we came, Samphire," I say to him. "Now that you're with me, it doesn't hurt to remember. I know you don't understand, but thank you." I give him a big kiss on his nose before he has time to avoid me.

And I make a heart out of small stones on the ground, in case the fairies are watching.

Chapter Sixteen

"You *promised*!" Ed is pulling my arm, trying to get me out of bed.

"It's six thirty in the morning," I moan, my eyes coming to focus on my alarm clock.

"You said stables then picnic," he whispers sternly in my face. His breath smells of chocolate cereal with marshmallows. He must have had breakfast already.

"It's Saturday. I don't need to be there until nine." I plunge my face back into my pillow. This is too much for Ed. He jumps on top of my duvet and starts bouncing. My bed lurches and squeaks in protest.

"Mom said last night that we've got to make the sandwiches, *lazy bones*," he shouts. I think there must have been a lot of additives in the chocolate cereal.

Resistance is pointless. I put my hands up in

surrender. My mattress heaves a sigh of relief as the onslaught stops.

"Remind me why it's a good thing to have a little brother," I say, wriggling out from under his weight, swinging my legs over the side of my bed and onto my purple rug.

" 'Cause I'm a bibble-bobble diggle-doggle magic-woggle super-blooper *champion of the world*!" he answers, trying to do a shoulder stand on my rumpled bedding and collapsing in giggles.

I shake my head. Ed's antics are too much at this time of the morning. I'm used to getting up on my own, at my own pace. Peace and quiet. The sound of my bike tires on the wet lane on the way to the stables. Samphire's song when he hears me approaching. The other horses murmuring, and the scraping of hooves on box stall floors.

I'm often the first to arrive. It's my favorite time of day, just me and all the animals adjusting to the new morning, shaking off the haze of sleep. I tell Samphire about the classes I'm enduring at school. He munches his breakfast and noses his bucket around, immune to the horrors of English essays and French verbs. I wish I could swap places with him sometimes. He would end up in the principal's office in no time, though, and not just for pooing in the classroom. His report would read: "Headstrong, boisterous, noisy, inattentive, a nightmare to teach. However, he is very good at running and will be an asset to the cross-country team."

As I pass Mom's open door, I glance in and see that she's still asleep, her hair spread out in a halo around her head. It's a nice image; Mom the angel. My memory suddenly produces another image, of Dad next to her, limbs spread untidily, bare chest protruding from the duvet (he only ever slept in his boxer shorts). We used to creep into the room, Ed and I, right up to the bed, and burrow between them, nestling into the warmth between their bodies.

"Permission to board, squadron leader," Ed would say. It was a phrase he learned very young, when he was negotiating the potty. He and Dad would salute each other before and after every maneuver.

"Permission granted," Dad would reply sleepily, half-peering at us through long, dark lashes. "But no wiggling, or I'll push the pilot eject button."

Pilot eject is not working. Repeat, pilot eject is not working...Dad's last words, recorded by the control deck on the aircraft carrier *Cronos*, patrolling the blue waters of the Gulf. Oh, memory, why do you do this? My heart suddenly beats in my chest so insistently I hear myself gasp a little. I need to focus on something else quickly to avoid the dizzy spell that usually follows. I wiggle my fingers and toes fast and hard and feel the tingle of a blood rush. It seems to have worked. I find myself breathing out slowly.

I blink twice and the vision of Mom and Dad together vanishes. I see only Mom, breathing softly, curled into soft folds of white linen on one side of the king-size bed, the book she has been reading still open next to her, where Dad should be. As if she senses me, her eyes open and she gives me a little wave.

"Trot on, Whinny," instructs Ed, his hands on my lower back.

"Don't push it," I warn him. I'm regretting saying today would be a good day for Ed to try aerobatics with his plane and for the three of us to eat lunch on the beach. For one thing, it's October. Ed assured me all week that today would be fine, according to the predictions on the weather site.

"Sunny face," he kept saying, dragging me to the computer and pointing to the yellow smiley suns over Hampshire on the chart. After several days of "maybe," Mom had a quiet word and told me it wasn't fair to make Ed wait any longer for his first aerobatic flight in front of an audience. It was to be a family occasion, complete with several layers of clothes, thermoses of soup, and a blanket to sit on.

I'm really happy for Ed that he has the plane of his dreams, which arrived in a long brown box and took him several weeks to learn to fly. He's been in his element, stretched out on the newspapers covering the cold, concrete floor of the garage—nimble fingers adjusting intricate parts, his tongue poking out to the left, the way it does when he's concentrating.

I can't tell him that I have this waking nightmare about Dad plummeting into the sea and that looking at any flying craft at all—even hearing an engine—can trigger it. I'm not sure how Mom feels, but I think it would be better all around if Ed liked collecting stamps instead.

Chapter Seventeen

In the summer, the bay is packed with tourists, like ants swarming on a perfectly curved banana. Out of season, it's almost deserted, apart from the occasional dog walker or angler digging up worms. It's where Dad and I rode and raced and ribbed each other. Looking at this golden horseshoe of a beach, I realize it's the last place I remember being happy and totally worry-free.

We all decided it was the best place for Ed to put his plane through its paces. Mom was very sensitive when we discussed it, asking me if I felt ready to come back here. I think I must be, because I found myself whispering in Samphire's ear that I would bring him to the bay one day, if he was very, very good, so that he could experience the gallop of his life.

"This is an exact replica of the combat plane that

took on the German Luftwaffe above southern England in the Battle of Britain in 1940," explained Ed, reading from his instruction leaflet as we tramped over pebbles and up and down the beach in search of exactly the right spot with the least wind resistance for the Spitfire's first aerial mission.

"You'd better go back a little," he advises now. He's wearing a black wool beanie hat, four layers under his coat, and a pair of jeans two sizes too big, but he still manages to look cute. Ten meters from his lumpy, ten-year-old frame, the Spitfire is positioned for takeoff.

Mom and I, who have helped Ed flatten the "runway" by jumping up and down a long strip of damp sand in our wellies, obey Ed's orders and move farther up the beach. Mom grabs my arm and cuddles it tightly as Ed gives us the thumbs-up sign and gazes down at his radio-controlled handset.

A sputter and a low, choking rumble. The propeller is turning, gathering speed. Ed shrieks and jumps up and down. Mom and I exchange glances, big grins on our faces. The Spitfire begins to edge forward, fuselage wobbling slightly over worm mounds we didn't spot. The painted pilot inside looks dwarfed by the one-and-a-half-meter camouflaged wingspan on either side of him.

There's a sudden spurt of speed, and the plane propels itself into the air, wings lurching to the left, taking the craft in a circle over our heads. Not *that* far over our heads, really. Mom and I both duck instinctively.

"Sorry!" yells Ed. He's sending the Spitfire south over the sand and toward the sea—the tide is way out. He turns it to the right and brings it lower to skim along over the rippling shoreline. He makes it bank steeply and follow an arc in the sky. Mom and I are holding our breath; disaster could strike any moment and Ed's dream could end in scattered wreckage.

Somehow, miraculously, the plane stays airborne, responding to the signals from Ed's handset. Mostly, he keeps it level, in between difficult maneuvers, spins, and loops. After several minutes, it's descending, its undercarriage wheels lowered, and it makes a speedy but perfect landing, coming to rest on the sand about fifty meters from Ed, who turns and raises his fist in triumph.

"Yaaaaaargh!" he shouts, doing a cartwheel but ending in a crumpled heap. When we reach him, he has extended his arms and legs, like a star, and his smile stretches from ear to ear.

"Did it," he states. There's relief in his voice. And excitement. And absolute happiness.

"Well done, you," says Mom, offering him a hand up and giving his damp, sandy frame a big hug.

"You're an ace pilot, Teddy," I tell him, pulling his ears.

"Leave me alone, Stick," he giggles.

We take some photos: Ed with his plane, saluting; me and Ed with his plane; Mom and Ed with his plane; the Spitfire (from all angles); me and Mom, pretending to be asleep on the beach.

We drink the hot soup from the thermos, eat the rolls and cupcakes and tease Mom about the pickle mustache on her top lip. Despite the damp cold, which is starting to seep into our bones, we feel great. It's been the best day. Mom looks radiant. Her eyes are bluer than I've ever seen.

And despite my heart being in my mouth a couple of times, watching the Spitfire plunge, I haven't felt weird or panicky. Maybe those bad times are finally leaving me alone?

"Last one to the plane is a rotten egg," Mom announces, setting off down the beach with her arms out on either side of her. Ed follows, making plane nosediving noises. I'm halfway through my granola bar, and running and swallowing isn't a great idea, so I stay put and watch them twirling on the sand so fast they make themselves dizzy.

Ed reaches the plane and proclaims that Mom is a "stinky, rotten egg." Together, they carry the plane back up the beach, joking with each other all the way.

Behind them, high above the skyline, a cotton-wool cloud has wisps of white trailing from its sides, silver slivers, dazzling in the sun. Maybe it's a sign from Dad, letting us know he approves. Maybe it's just a cloud. I take a video of it on my phone. When I play it back, the brightness has obscured the picture. There are silhouettes of two people carrying a plane. All you can hear is Ed laughing.

Chapter Eighteen

"Oh, that's so *gross*!" I'm standing directly behind Samphire, three strands of white hair in my hand, getting a braiding lesson from Rachel. My horse has decided, at this precise moment, to lift his tail and deposit half a bucketful of manure on my boots. Rachel and I scoot to the door, holding our noses.

"That's what he thinks of our makeover," says Rachel, smiling. Samphire looks at us with wide eyes full of mischief. "Maybe it's time to have a hot chocolate and a bite to eat before we regroup?" she suggests.

"Yeah," I agree. "Breakfast! Great idea."

It's a tradition at the stables that Sue cooks breakfast for the workers on Sunday mornings. I've mucked out four horses since arriving at eight o'clock and hosed down the yard. I've also managed to give Rambo an extra special grooming. I can see him tossing his mane in his stable, proud of his makeover! It's ten thirty now and my stomach is aching with hunger—maybe that's why I was all fingers and thumbs with the braiding. I've already learned one important lesson, though. Samphire does not like his tail being brushed or tugged on. As we close the stable door after us, he seems to be muttering under his breath.

"I heard that," I tell him. He turns and stretches his graceful head, nuzzling my outstretched hand. His tongue rasps over my palm, leaving a trail of slimy saliva. It's either his idea of a kiss or an attempt to locate some treats. "Thanks, Sam. I'm coming back, so don't think you're off the hook."

Rachel and I wolf down the fried egg, bacon, and sausage sandwiches, which Sue hands us on paper plates as we enter the tiny kitchen at the back of the office. We're the last to join the breakfast gang. Grace, Ellie, and Ashleigh are perching on the office desk, their hands cupped around steaming mugs of hot chocolate.

There's a welcoming fug of steam and heat in the small space. Only a short time ago, I would have taken my food and gone somewhere else to eat, not wanting to feel like the odd one out among the "cool" crew. Thanks to Rachel, I'm feeling more a part of things here. Having Samphire has given me a new status too. I'm an owner now, not just a volunteer, and I work to pay as much of his livery as I can.

I'm licking the ketchup off my fingers and my eyes are focused on the notice board, which has several pieces of paper pinned to it. Some relate to feeds for the horses with special asterisks for those on medication. There are lists of rides booked for today and the coming week and a thick health and safety document hanging on a string from a drawing pin, which we're supposed to learn by heart. At the bottom, in the right-hand corner, there's a flyer about the Oakhurst cross-country race in the new year.

"Why don't you go for it?" asks Rachel, observing my gaze. "Take Samphire through his paces."

"Do you think we're ready?" I ask, anxiety mixed with sudden excitement.

"It's a few weeks away. I can help you prepare," replies Rachel, eyebrows raised, willing me to agree.

"Wow," I say quietly, considering the enormity of the challenge of taking Sam over a two-mile course with more than twenty testing jumps.

"Say yes," encourages Grace. "He'll get a rosette just for looking beautiful."

"OK," I hear myself whispering. "As long as he doesn't have to have a braid!"

I'm riding my bike as if propelled by rocket fuel, pedaling along the lane that leads to my house. Water droplets from the recent shower splash on my head and neck from the overhanging branches. My tires swish through the sheet of liquid, splattering mud onto my boots and jodhpurs.

The afternoon air tastes damp. My nose breathes in the musty fungal fragrance of mulched leaves and earth, decaying bark, and the black water of the still stream by the lane's edge, which is steaming gently like a potion in a cauldron.

Winter sun is poking at the soil with its long, straight fingers, making the stagnant ground stir with new energy. I think Samphire has done the same for me. I'm riding up our path now, desperate to tell Mom and Ed about the race. I lean my bike against the garage and run in big bounds to the back door. I kick off my dirty boots on the mat and pull down the handle at the same time, eager to get into the kitchen. There's no sign of life, or the snacks that are usually on the table at this time.

"*Mom! Teddy!*" I yell as I run through the oven-warmed room to the hallway.

I jump as I crash into Mom, with her finger to her lips. She's on the phone. Her face looks drawn and tired. Ed is sitting on the stairs, holding his favorite teddy. He's a strange gray color. His lips are translucent and the rims around his eyes are purple. His breathing is wheezy and his shoulders are hunched forward, making him look very small.

"Thank you. Yes. We'll come right away," says Mom into the receiver before pressing the End Call button and replacing the phone on its cradle.

"What's going on?" I ask, breathless from adrenaline and sudden fear.

"Ed's got to go to the hospital, Jodie," explains Mom quietly.

"Thing is," says Ed. "There's blood in my pee."

Chapter Nineteen

"Did you bring your magic wand, Stick?" asks Ed quietly. He is lying in a bed in the medical assessment unit of the hospital, with tubes coming out of his arm and his chest. The machine that is pumping fluid and painkillers from a suspended clear sac into his body bleeps every so often. His blood samples, taken when we arrived, are being analyzed. Mom is with the doctor.

"You won't need a wand, Teddy," I tell him, squeezing his small hand a bit to hard. "I've brought a time-travel machine in my pocket."

"Cool." He grins. "Maybe it could take me to the future where no one gets kidney disease." Ed isn't quite meeting my eyes. I notice that his face is puffier than when we arrived two hours ago. It also has a yellowish tinge, matching the flowery curtains that are pulled around his bed, giving us some privacy in the busy ward.

"These are a bit like those tablecloths Dad used to make us tents in the garden. Do you remember?" I ask him, nodding to the screens of fabric dotted with daisies and bees.

"A.C. was so mad that we were using them as walls for our fort," Ed responds. A.C. is our abbreviation for Auntie Connie. "Madeiran lace, *handmade*," he says, imitating her earnest and put-out tone.

Mom says that her older sister's heart is always in the right place, but her affections lean more toward creatures in distress than young children.

"So, Edward," continues my brother, still mimicking A.C. "Just think to yourself, 'Bother! Life has dealt me a bad hand, but I'm going to say fiddle-de-dee and make the best of it.'" He makes one of her serious faces, eyes wide and nostrils slightly flared like a sheep. We're both giggling. Ed's a bit breathless. I pass him a glass of water from his bedside table.

"You're going to be all right, Teddy," I reassure him. "Maybe you just need some more blood. You did a lot of running around with the plane yesterday."

"Can I see the pics again?" asks Ed. The camera is still in my pocket. I always carry it around in case I want to take a photo of Samphire, which I do pretty much every day. I click it to life and scroll back through the shots of Sam rolling on his back in the frost this morning, trying hard to get the padded winter coat off. Ed sighs and tuts.

"Hang on," I tell him. "There, found it." I pass the camera to him so that he can see himself holding his prized Spitfire with Mom. I lean forward and help him zoom in so that he can look at their big smiles.

"Very good looking," he comments, nodding.

"Vain!" I tease.

"The plane, Whinny, duh," he replies with a pained expression. His gaze focuses on the frames as he clicks between them. For a moment, he seems lost and sad.

"We'll take it flying again really soon," I say. Ed just shrugs.

Mom appears through the curtains. She sits carefully on the edge of the bed and takes a little breath before speaking.

"OK. Well, they think we're going to need to go for more tests. You're not showing signs of infection, but the doctors here have been speaking to the specialist kidney team and they want to take an organ tissue sample to see what's going on. They're making arrangements to transfer us in an ambulance." Mom touches Ed's arm lightly and gives him a big smile. "They are the best team in the country. We'll be in good hands."

Ed gives her a single nod to let her know he's taken in the information.

We all sit in silence for a moment. Then Mom looks at me. "Jodie, I'm going to ask Auntie Connie to come and take care of you, just while Ed has his tests and until we know what's happening."

"I'm coming with you," I announce, shocked that she could think otherwise.

"The ambulance can only take one other passenger," explains Mom gently. "And there will be a lot of waiting around up there. Samphire needs you here. I'll tell you everything that's happening. I think we'll be back before you know it."

"Can I stay with Rachel?" I spurt out. My brain is in panic mode. I can't bear to think of being separated from Mom and Ed. The idea of A.C. flying down and "taking care" of me fills me with complete dread.

Mom considers this. "I could ask Rachel's mom if you like," she says. "Hopefully, it will only be for a couple of days."

I give Mom Rachel's number. She takes her cell phone off to the nearest corridor away from the ward where phone calls are allowed.

"You get to miss school," I say to my brother, pretending like I'm jealous.

"The evil Ice Woman will track me down," Ed replies.

"We won't tell her," I promise.

There's a tear sliding slowly down Ed's right cheek. "Something in my eye, Stick. Got a tissue?"

I feel in my pocket and find a crumpled, used one that smells like horse. I tear off a corner and pass it to Ed, who stares at it, perplexed.

"What am I supposed to do with that? Take a shrinking potion and blow my nose?" Ed tuts again before lifting the bedsheet toward his face and rubbing hard, removing all traces of blubbering. "Probably just an eyelash," he says, not meeting my gaze.

Chapter Twenty

Everything is dark. I'm surrounded by flickering, warm hair. My head is buried deep into a gray horse flank. My eyes are closed. Samphire is standing very still, staring at the full moon. From far away, he must look like a ghost horse in the mist, rising from the frost-rigid field. His left rear fetlock is tilted, the tip of his shoe resting on the ground. We breathe in unison. I imagine seeing the world through his eyes. I want to think of nothing but food for my belly, a warm shelter, an open trail to explore, and the freedom of the winds.

There would be no images of blood and tubes and machines. No charts and pills and fluids. No acrid smell of bodily functions, antibacterial soap, and cleaning agents. No doctors in huddles, comparing notes.

Mom called and said the hospital is very modern with great paintings on the walls and a brilliant play area with computers. Ed is in a small ward of eight kids. She can sleep next to him on a special pull-out bed. They've had some tea and everyone is really friendly.

"When will you be home?" I asked at least four times.

"We'll see the medical team in the morning. I'll know a bit more then," she replied. "Jode, I need you to email my feature to Rupert at the magazine, can you do that? He's getting one of the editors to finish it off."

"Yup," I reply. "I'll ask Rachel's mom if we can stop at home. I'm sure she won't mind."

"Thanks. You're wonderful. I'm sending a hug. Here it comes…"

My phone is buzzing. There's a text: *Stick, am so glad u r not on the pull-out bed. Cld not stand the snoring. Great hosptl. There r planes on my duvet + a jet mobile. Howd they know??? Played cards 4 money w drs. I won $2. I have to pee in cardboard thingie. Theres a kid here clld Ravi. He got 1 eye. Hope u r OK. bfn :) xxx*

Ed never sends kisses. He must be really scared. My chest tightens at this thought and a lump forms in my throat. Before I know it, my nose is streaming. I reach for a tissue and find the crumpled bit from earlier. Just seeing it makes me want to cry, but no sound comes. Samphire turns his head and looks at me with unblinking eyes. Then he nuzzles my hand, my neck, my cheek. He's trying to comfort me. His whiskers are quite spiky and tickle my face. I'm smiling now, although my ribs are hurting with sadness. I lean against Sam and let my cold fingers text a reply: *Sleepg w S in stable. Don't tell Mom. Kidding! Going home w R soon. Will b strange. Hurry up + get better lol xxx* ☺ *ps when u were little u peed in bin so cardboard thingie no prob!*

The full moon is bathing the whole field in cool, clear light. Rabbits are skittering about in the far corner, nibbling blades of grass and sitting upright in turn. The three other horses nearby are all standing still, like Samphire, facing the light as if it's pulling them toward it, drawing them in. They seem caught in a moon spell, watching, listening, alert.

"Bedtime, Sam," I tell him, stroking his ear, which is tensed forward, straining for any sounds. I slip my hand under the cheek strap of his halter and ease his head toward me. He resists at first. Maybe he and all the nighttime creatures are waiting for a message from the universe.

Maybe there's a special magic, a portal to dreams, and the animals see it. Just in case, I make a wish, for Ed and Mom and me, and I blow it softly from the palm of my hand, up into the blackness, to space. To Dad, whose breath and laughter and words are out there somewhere.

"Ouch, get off my foot, you oaf!" I command Samphire, who is protesting and causing me acute pain at the same time. A grumble travels from his throat and comes in snatches through his opening and closing lips. It's a strange conversation, but the meaning is clear. He's telling me off.

"I hear you, grumpy. But you're going back to your stable, no argument." This time, he walks with me without hesitation and without me leading him. He stays close, almost in step, and he waits for me to open and then close the gate before continuing down the concrete path to the yard.

I prepared his stable earlier, so when I close the door and run the bolt across, I expect him to put his nose in his bucket as usual. But he turns and faces me, neck arched and proud, his eyes full of moonlight. Again, the grumble from his throat, the snatches of horse-speak, more quietly this time.

"What is it?" I ask him, stroking his neck.

"He's telling you everything's going to be OK," says Rachel, who is waiting patiently, my overnight bag stuffed with schoolbooks and PE uniform on her shoulder.

Chapter Twenty-One

There's a high-pitched squeal, the clash of metal on metal. Then comes a jolt, which makes my body lurch and we're thrust from the darkness of the tunnel into the gloomy light of late morning. Through the smeary window, my eyes follow rows of terraced houses, so close to the train track that they seem to be breathing on it; billboards with white-toothed, smiling families; blocks of apartments with lines of washing hanging on narrow balconies; cars bumper to bumper parked in long lines, street after street after street.

I'm coming, Ed. I'm on my way.

Soon, to my right, there is a disused power station—an ugly, brown castle of bricks with broken windows. The train has slowed and is snaking between office blocks and the backs of superstores. Some of the buildings are so high, they seem to reach the sky. As the train crosses the river, I notice new apartment blocks, shining with polished glass and chrome opulence.

The people here live like hamsters, stacked in cages. The idea of it makes me shudder.

We're approaching the station. Mom is meeting me there and taking me to St. Saviour's to be with Ed. Everything she told me last night is swirling in my brain. It's hard to take it in.

Ed is very sick. His right kidney is giving up and his left one isn't strong enough to do the job of both. He needs a transplant urgently. The kidney team is trying to find a match.

I feel bug-eyed due to lack of sleep. I was counting the hours and minutes until Rachel's mom was able to take me to the station and see me onto the train. My stomach is complaining too. Someone farther down the carriage is eating a burger; the smell makes me feel nauseous and hungry at the same time. I only had a bite of toast with butter earlier—I couldn't force myself to eat any more.

I thought, until yesterday, that our family had had its share of bad luck and sadness. But now we're back on our life raft, paddling for survival.

Ed's situation is complicated. He has a rare tissue type, which is why Mom and I were discounted as donors when he was first diagnosed. The doctors said it would be like "looking for a needle in a haystack" if the time came to find a matching organ. In my book, that means very difficult, but not impossible. You just need to search very thoroughly.

But there's an even greater problem in this case. Our enemy isn't really Ed's bad kidney, or the immune system that has suddenly failed him. The doctors have said it's something you can't touch, see, or taste. Time. Why do people say it's "running out," when it has no legs?

We are in a "race against time," according to the consultant. That's why I'm here. To help Ed win.

Mom is waiting on the platform as the train pulls in. I have to line up to get out of the carriage behind a granny with a wheelie suitcase, a kid in a stroller, two women in saris, and a man with a cello in a case. But soon enough, Mom's wrapping her arms around me and holding me tight. Something goes crunch. I look down and there's a paper bag full of freshly made cookies between us.

"Caramel and milk-chocolate chip," she tells me. "How was the journey?"

"Fine," I answer, biting into a cookie. Mom has her hands on my shoulders and her eyes are a bit watery.

"They've found a kidney for Ed," she says softly.

"That's so great!" I exclaim, crumbs showering onto the platform.

"Yes. It's amazing really. It all happened so fast, it's hard to take in," continues Mom, her face taut with anxiety and tiredness. I don't suppose she's been sleeping well in the ward.

She's guiding me across the concourse. Buses, cars,

people cross my line of vision, a blur of action and noise. We're swept along in the gray tide of business suits and overcoats. The air is biting cold.My face and hands are numb. Mom isn't saying a lot and her expression is starting to make me very nervous.

She hails a taxi and in moments we're sitting in the back of a cab, edging through traffic, still south of the river. It's started to rain. The windshield wipers squeak and shudder as we pass through an unfamiliar landscape. A city in which my brother now faces surgery.

I feel like there's a blade in my belly, turning very slowly.

Mom's cell phone starts to ring. She reaches into her bag and answers it with a curt "Yes?" instead of her usual friendly "Hello." She listens, says, "Thank you for letting me know," and ends the call.

"It's on its way. Ed can have surgery later today." Mom squeezes my hand. "Everything will be all right," she tries to reassure me.

Chapter Twenty-Two

"Heyyyy, Sticko," says Ed, giving me a small wave, his hand only just raised from the side of the bed.

"Hey, little brother," I reply, giving his fingers a gentle tug.

Ed, who looks smaller and more fragile than I remember, has been sleeping all afternoon. Any minute now, he's going down to the operating room for surgery. His new kidney, which has been transported by air ambulance, is approaching the helipad on top of the hospital.

"Cool. What kind of helicopter is it?" he asks when Mom tells him what's happening.

"A very fast one," I reply. He gives me this look that tells me I'm an idiot for not knowing the model and type. Then his eyes droop a bit. That must be the injection he had a little while ago.

"Spitfire needs…handset can't be…not outside…"
Ed is mumbling, agitated.

"We'll take care of your plane, darling. Just think
about how well you'll feel after this operation. How
fast you'll be able to run. All the sports you'll be able
to do—soccer, swimming…" Mom soothes, her voice
quiet and calm.

"Riding," I add.

"No way," Ed smiles before fading into a deep,
medicated sleep.

When Mom and I look up, two nursing orderlies
are waiting to wheel his bed to the operating room.
Mom gives Ed a kiss and we both walk with him until
we get to the elevator. When the doors close, I grab
Mom's hand. She looks a bit shell-shocked.

"It'll be OK, Mom," I tell her. "Doctors do this
all the time. Ed's going to be eating and drinking
tomorrow and could be back to school in a couple
of months."

"I know," she replies. I notice that the bottom half

of her face is smiling at me, but her eyes are fixed and fearful. "I wish Dad was here," she adds softly. I don't know what to say, so I squeeze her hand. "It's going to be a very long two hours," she sighs.

"Why don't you get your mom a nice cup of tea, Jodie?" suggests Lizzie, the staff nurse in charge of the surgical ward, gently leading us toward the family room. "There are snacks and magazines and stuff, so you can stretch out and relax a bit. And if you need anything or want to ask any questions, I'm here."

"Thank you," says Mom. And moments later we're alone in the cream-painted room with low red sofas, a pay phone, a kitchen area, a TV, a playpen full of toys, and a white tinsel Christmas tree with a star on the top.

I start to make tea as I need something to do. When I hand mom a steaming mug, I can see she's been crying.

"Sorry, Jodie," she says, blowing her nose. "It's just, one minute, everything seems great and fine and dandy, and the next...It all goes down, like a pack of cards."

"It won't, Mom," I say, giving her a hug. She looks at me and there is such pain in her face. My heart is beating so loudly I can hear its thud in my ears. "Is there something you're not telling me?"

Mom's eyes are filling up again. I take her hand and she puts her other one on top of mine.

"I had a call from Rupert. The magazine has to make cuts so I've lost my two days a week."

"That sucks," I say, holding her hand. It feels weird that Mom is talking to me like an adult. "You'll be able to get other work, though."

"I won't be able to earn anything like the same amount from freelance features. And I can't look for another contract until Ed is completely better," explains Mom.

"I'll get another job," I suggest. Mom shakes her head.

"I'll get my head around it," she says, wiping her eyes.

"We'll manage. We always do." Somehow, those words are sounding a bit hollow.

"Yes," she agrees. "We'll have to make some changes, though." Mom isn't meeting my gaze.

And suddenly, my brain feels as if it is vibrating to a rhythm, an insistent drumming sound. I close my eyes and all I can see is Samphire, galloping toward me. He's trying to reach me, but the space between us is widening. He's whinnying his song urgently with panic in his eyes. I'm shouting his name, but no sound comes out of my mouth. As I watch, he becomes smaller, more distant. He's disappearing behind plumes of dust.

I open my eyes with a start. In the last few minutes, I have felt my world shift to a new, dark place. There's an idea stalking my thoughts like a shadow. I try to focus on Ed, but it is lurking, waiting for a moment to jump into my consciousness.

Mom and I sit in silence. She leafs through a magazine with celebrities on the front, all big smiles, boobs, and white teeth. We watch the minutes tick by on the white clock above the door. Five minutes. Ten minutes. I want to fast-forward everything to the point where we take Ed home and life is normal again and the money situation is miraculously solved.

We watch a game show on TV, not responding to the questions at all, sitting like dumb stuffed dolls. The canned audience laughter sounds too loud, like the frenzied cry of seagulls.

We jump when some metal trays fall from a passing trolley in the corridor outside and freeze when a kid of about six runs into the family room, laughing and pulling a wooden dog on a rope behind her. Her mass of red curls tumbles over her navy coat.

"This is Geoffrey," she tells us proudly.

"He's very nice," answers Mom.

"He does tricks, watch," she instructs us. "Sit, Geoffrey. Good dog. See?" She's suspending the rope so that the dog's bottom is resting on the carpet. "Do you want to give him a cookie?"

"Yes, please," says Mom, offering him one from the plate. The girl snatches it and runs toward the door with Geoffrey bumping along behind.

"My sister is sick but she is going to get better. Bye," she calls, giving us a wave from the door, which closes softly behind her.

"She was cute," says Mom, relaxing a little.

I don't reply. My thoughts are racing. Images of Ed flash through my mind and my brain is still pounding, but it's hooves I can hear. And suddenly a face flashes across my consciousness, with indistinct features and colorless hair. A face that had a name.

"Who is Ed's kidney coming from?" I blurt out. Mom pauses before she answers.

"A teenage girl. No details." We're both quiet for a few minutes, thinking about this sad kid who is weirdly, strangely becoming integrated into our family; who's helping my brother have a new life; who gave her consent to organ donation, never believing the day would ever come. I'm glad we don't know her name or what she looked like.

"Everything's going well," says Lizzie, poking her head around the door. "Ed should be back in recovery in about fifteen minutes. I'll keep you posted." She beams and disappears. There is a girly *woof, woof* nearby, so we know that Geoffrey is listening and wants us to know he approves.

I think again about Ed, who is little but so brave. He doesn't moan about any of it—the transfusions, the hours sitting at the clinic, the lessons he has to make up, the sports he hasn't been able to do.

I'll follow his example. He and Mom need me to be strong and there for them in every way. The idea that's been gnawing at the back of my mind is emerging from the shadows. I'm beginning to see it clearly now—and I can't hide from it. There's something I must do...

There will have to be some changes.

Lizzie is back and her big smile says it all. "They're very pleased with him," she confirms. "Once Ed has been moved to intensive care you can go and be with him."

Mom gives me a big hug. She's shaking. It must be a mixture of relief and worry. Ed is out of danger for now, although it will be a tough few weeks while he gets used to the anti-rejection drugs and his new organ.

"I'm so glad you were here today," she says in my ear. "I'm really proud of how you're handling this."

"I missed French," I reply with a shrug and as much of a grin as I can muster. It's lucky Mom can't see into my brain, where a beautiful gray horse is now running for his life, no place of safety in sight.

Chapter Twenty-Three

Grooming Samphire has taken twice as long as usual. Every sweep of the brush over his coat has been heavy and slow, so different from my usual routine. He keeps nickering and nibbling my sleeve, sensing that something is wrong.

I lean against him and let my head rest on his neck. He smells musty after a night in the stable, but his warmth is a comfort. My hand is stroking his flank, which quivers. He knows that very soon I will saddle him up for a ride, and his body is taut with anticipation.

"I'm so sorry, Sam," I whisper. He whinnies a reply and rubs his face against mine. "But I promise you, when everything is OK again, I'll find you and bring you home."

I told Mom that I was going to sell Samphire on

the night she brought Ed home from hospital. I waited until he was asleep, because I don't want him to know. I said my mind was made up, because it would mean Mom can have her money back and won't have to find an extra lump sum each month to subsidize Samphire's livery. We have to focus on getting Ed well again and that has to be more important than anything else.

Mom didn't say anything. She listened, held me tight, and cried silent tears. After some time, she said just two words: "Thank you."

It was so hard telling Rachel and Sue. I knew they would try to come up with some options to help me keep Samphire. Sue offered to keep him as a riding horse until I was able to reclaim him. Rachel's lovely family said they would pay for his keep at the stables temporarily.

The trouble is, we need the lump sum from his sale to keep us going until Mom can work again. And she would never accept financial help from Rachel's parents or Sue. Even if Sam could stay at the stables, with his sensitive nature, he wouldn't like the change and he'd find it hard to adapt to being a riding horse with lots of new handlers. He might even become unrideable again or ill. It would be the hardest thing in the world to see his spirit broken. At least if he goes to a good home, he'll have a better life than that.

A decision is one thing. Making it happen is totally different. I don't think I've eaten a whole meal since that night—my stomach is permanently knotted up. I've had to tell Ed I've got a bug. He's really worried about me, which is crazy. He's the one who needs all our TLC.

"You're like a stick, Stick," he said to me this morning.

"What's a stick stick?" I replied.

"It's like a mini pretzel, only twice as thin."

"Don't worry, as soon as I'm better I'm going to eat a whole bag of doughnuts," I promised.

"Maybe you've got a tarantula in your belly that is eating your food," he suggested helpfully. Ever since he watched *Spider Attack* on DVD, he's had them on the brain.

"That must be it. Thanks for the diagnosis, Teddy."

He looked at me through narrowed eyes; I think he's getting suspicious. He's already asked Mom why she's not going downtown. She told him that her work is on hold while he's recovering, but he's clever—it won't take him long to put two and two together once I'm doing fewer hours at the stable.

Samphire is pawing at his straw. I've been daydreaming and not in a good way. Mom said I should try to live for the moment and enjoy every precious minute I have with him.

I'm doing my best, but I wish with all my heart I could hold back time.

Chapter Twenty-Four

"Come on, boy, let's go," I say to Samphire, urging him into a fast canter. The ground beneath his feet is squishy with water after days of rain. Today, sun is dancing around the edges of the clouds and the puddles on the woodland tracks are silver mirrors to the sky.

It's Christmas Eve. Ed is making progress but he needs dialysis again while he adjusts to his new kidney. That's not unusual after a transplant, his surgeon assured us. But I think Ed's disappointed. He's been very quiet, even when he had a couple of friends over for his birthday last week. I know Mom's worried, but she's busying herself with preparations for the Christmas lunch tomorrow. We're keeping it low-key as my secret is weighing heavily on us both.

Sam is skittish and difficult, sensing my distracted

mood. He flinches at the sight of bushes and almost bolts when confronted by a rabbit darting from behind the stump of a dead tree.

"Shh, boy, careful now." I try to ease his nervousness with soothing strokes on his neck. He won't be calmed, though. This ride he knows so well is suddenly like foreign territory to him, every step a potential trap. I think he knows that everything is about to change. When I saddled him this morning, I couldn't look him in the eye. I feel like a betrayer.

All around us, a blanket of orange-brown ferns lies heavily across the soggy undergrowth. The hidden beginnings of life beneath are waiting for warmer days to begin their ascent. I wish it would be winter forever, though. Once spring begins, Samphire will be gone, taking my hopes for happiness with him.

The advertisement that we're going to place in January is already drafted on my desk at home:

Beautiful, gray part-Arab stallion, 3 years old, 15 hands. Spirited, suitable for experienced rider. Event

potential, willing jumper. Family illness forces sale.
$2,000.

In a few days, I will be entering these words, my name, and my number into a box on my computer screen, and with a click of the mouse, Samphire's details will be added to the "For Sale" section in the next edition of *Riding* magazine. He will never know that he's becoming more valuable with every new skill he learns; that to me, he is priceless.

Each morning, when I wake up, I think the whole situation is just a bad dream. I blink and rub my eyes. The first thing I focus on is the photo of Samphire by my bed. In seconds, my memory starts to function, sending an aching sadness from my stomach to my throat.

Then I see Ed, who on a good day will be sliding down the banisters, cleaning his beloved Spitfire, laughing like a loony over some stupid cartoon, his wild hair twisted into blond dreadlocks with pencils sticking out of them, and I feel guilty and ashamed.

"Sacrifice is about giving something up for a higher good," our principal said in the last assembly of the semester. She hoped we would sponsor a cow or donate money for school books in the third world instead of asking for presents. The boys made mooing noises and the Glossies turned up their noses at the idea of fewer presents of beauty products under the tree.

My eyes had stung, especially when she ended by saying, "It's not just about sharing your last chocolate, but the good intent in your heart." I wanted to yell that sacrifice is really about the big things in life, not just cows or books or candy or gifts wrapped up with ribbons. And that sometimes, it's a terrible choice.

"But it doesn't have to be forever," I say out loud, curling lower, willing Samphire to go faster. "I will come and find you, Sam, wherever you are, however long it takes."

Chapter Twenty-Five

"Hey, Jodie," says Rachel as she leads Rambo toward his stable. He's just back from an afternoon ride and steam is rising from his back. He has orange chunks in the corner of his mouth, the remains of a carrot given by his appreciative young rider.

"Hey," I say, mustering a smile and then busying myself with the currycomb on Sam's muddy legs to avoid further conversation. Rachel knows how hard I'm finding the situation. I wonder if she's seen the ad in *Riding*. She's so kind, but there's nothing she can say to cheer me up.

Samphire is nuzzling my boot, then my pocket, where the treats live. When I don't respond, he leans against me and his left foot stomps on my toes.

"Bad horse," I say, pushing him off. "You don't

get treats until I've finished brushing you. You know the rules."

"So handsome," says Rachel, appearing by my side. She strokes Sam's nose gently. He tosses his mane as if in agreement. "As soon as the field drains, we could try him on some jumps," she suggests. "What do you think?"

"No point," I shrug. My throat feels tight and dry.

"Any calls yet?" she asks. She must have seen the ad. I shake my head.

"It's so tough. I think you're being really brave," sighs Rachel sadly, her hand on Samphire's neck. She wouldn't say that if she'd seen me punching my pillow at night.

"I'll get him back," I state.

"Good," says Rachel, giving Sam a kiss on his nose. "We don't want to let you go for long, gorgeous," she whispers in his ear before moving away with a thoughtful, backward glance.

There's no going back now, Sam. The part of my

brain that kept telling me I could always change my mind has just realized that it's no use pretending. These will be our last days together, unless a miracle comes or Mom wins the lotto. *I can't believe that I was lucky enough to find you and now I'm losing you.* The unfairness of it all is twisting and gnawing at my guts. The ache is turning to constant pain.

Chapter Twenty-Six

"Whassup, Stick?" asks Ed, his face two inches from mine. He smells of toast and honey and bacon. Mom must be attempting pancakes. You really need maple syrup for those. At least she didn't use marmalade.

"Hey, Teddy," I say sleepily. I was awake most of the night and only drifted off when it was getting light. My dreams are always the same—I'm riding Samphire, pursued by men in black cloaks with lassoes. I wince when I glimpse Ed's operation scar through his pajamas and suddenly imagine blood gushing through it, covering my bed in red gloop.

"Are you sick, Stick?" he persists, lifting my eyelids in turn. "Mom says because you're a teenager you need to sleep because that's when you do your *growing* but it's *nine o'clock* and Samphire needs his mush and I need some company and it's time you *got up*. Mom sent you a pancake. Look. Mmmmm."

Ed dangles the strange-shaped limp object under my nose with his fingers. It smells floury and sweet.

"Can't you go and glue something onto your plane," I respond a bit surly.

"Moody dudey," he declares. "Mom says that's because of your horse-mones."

"Look, shut up!" I snap. "Get off my bed and out of my room. I should be at the stables."

"You don't mean it," he teases, wrapping himself up in my duvet as I swing my feet onto the floor, stepping on the sad pancake and in the runny honey on the plate.

"I really *do*!" I yell, kicking the tray away and hopping out of my room toward the bathroom. Once inside, I slam the door and raise my sticky foot to the tap in the sink. Cold water gushes over it, sending the nerves into frenzy.

"Aaargh!" I exclaim. There is a soft knock. "What?" I answer.

"About you hating me," says a small voice.

"I don't hate you, Teddy," I answer more gently.

"I understand, it's OK."

"Why would I hate you?" I ask, busy drying my toes with the towel.

There is a neigh from the hallway and fingers making galloping sounds up and down the door. I find myself sliding down, leaning against it. I can hear Ed breathing, very close.

"I'm not stupid, Stick," says my brother. I'm hugging my knees under my chin. I feel so small. The toilet, sink, and bath look enormous from this angle.

"I didn't want Mom to tell you," I say.

"She didn't. I asked Dr. Devereux. He told me you were the best sister in the world. I couldn't argue 'cause I had a thing down my throat. Kidding. You are the B-E-S-T-E-S-T." There is an awkward silence between us. I think we are back to back, because I can feel the door vibrating when Ed breathes out.

"I've got a hundred dollars in my safe," he says after a while, certain that this will solve all our problems.

"That's two weeks' livery," I tell him.

"That horse eats too much," sighs Ed, his head flopping back with a thud. "Don't sell Samphire, Stick," he almost whispers. "Pleeeeeeease."

"I have to, Ed. We need the money. But I'm going to work really hard and buy him back as soon as I can."

"In six months?" Ed asks.

"Definitely," I say, crossing all my fingers, the way Ed and I do when we tell white lies.

"Are you crossing your fingers?" he asks. I untangle them immediately.

"Nope," I answer.

"Stick?"

"What?"

"I'm really sorry. I made you something. You don't have to like it." There is a scuffling noise and under the door Ed pushes a piece of paper, neatly folded into

168

a star shape with four pointed corners. There is a word written in different colored felt tip on each. They read, *I love you, sis.*

My body is shaking with sadness. No tears come, just a pain that holds my jaw rigid and my breath locked inside my chest.

"You have to come out now," says Ed.

"In a minute," I manage to reply.

"No, now, Stick. There's someone on the phone and Mom says it's for you."

Chapter Twenty-Seven

"Steady, Sam. I need you to stand still." I'm putting the last protective boot on my horse's restless legs, making sure that he's insulated from the hazards of being transported by trailer across the county.

It's the morning I've been dreading. The sky is gray-metal heavy. There's an icy north wind, carrying with it showers of sleet that clatter on the corrugated roof of the tack room. Outside Sam's stable, the yard is awash with brown water running off the fields. The red-brown sludge in the drainage ditch is causing a small stream to run down to the lane. The flood is like the lifeblood flowing from my heart.

I will always remember the searing pain of this moment as I look at Samphire, almost regal in his clean coat and polished halter, his oiled hooves and conditioned mane. His eyes are bright and watchful, his nostrils sniffing at the stormy January air. His ears flick back and forth, trying to pick up any sounds that will tell him what is happening next.

I snip a small clump of hair from under his forelock with my trimming scissors and put it in my pocket. I need to have something real left behind, something I can hold and smell. I'm already thinking I won't wash my jacket, with its smears of horse spit where Sam has probed for treats and tugged my collar. And these jodhpurs with their dark marks on the knees rubbed from his belly on our last ride through the forest, will go into my drawer as a precious memento.

"They're here," says Rachel, appearing by the door. "They're backing up."

The noise from the Land Rover reversing a horse box into the yard grinds in my brain. It sounds like a tank on maneuvers. It has its sights fixed on us and is approaching. There's nowhere for us to hide. Samphire whinnies and it must be a warning, as Rambo and several other horses reply with anxious snorts and neighs.

"Do you want me to load him?" asks Rachel, really concerned at the sight of my face, which must look like that painting *The Scream*, only worse.

"No," I reply, my voice an octave higher than usual, the sound strangled by the closing of my throat. "He'll feel less scared if I do it."

"I'm sorry, Samphire," I whisper for the thousandth time. The words don't seem like enough. "I promise you, I won't ride another horse—no one but you." I'm looking into his eyes as I say this, so he can see it's a solemn vow. There are voices outside and a sharp clang as the trailer door is lowered onto the ground. Footsteps, a deep cough that rasps behind ribs, a greeting from Rachel.

I pull the bolt on the stable door back angrily, my other trembling hand holding the halter rope. Sam senses that this isn't a normal exit from his safe haven and throws his head back in a jolt, backing away from me.

"He's being silly, Daddy," says the fifteen-year-old girl called Leila who has persuaded her father that a part-Arab stallion will fill the gap in her list of birthday presents. "He didn't do this the first time we came to see him," she adds, looking at me accusingly.

"He likes routine," I try to tell her. "Trailers frighten him."

"He'll have to get used to it," she replies. "I'm going to take him to lots of Pony Club events."

Leila doesn't seem like the same girl I met before. That girl was kind and full of smiles. That's why I agreed to sell Samphire to her.

"And if you decide to sell him, you'll call me, like you promised?" I'm taking every chance to remind Leila of the agreement we made when her dad handed me a check two weeks ago.

"Yes," she sighs, a bit irritated. Then her face softens. "I know this is really hard for you."

I just nod. "If you stand away a little, I'll bring him out." There's a knife in my guts, twisting . . .

I reach into my pocket and find some nuts, showing them to Sam, who is messing up the hay on the ground with his right hoof. "Look. Treats," I say gently. He snorts and takes two steps forward suspiciously. "Good boy. Now we're going into the yard. Come on. Quietly. Ssshhh. That's it. You can have them as soon as we get you up the ramp. Four more steps, Sam, just four more."

"Up you go!" says the father sternly, his hand on Samphire's flank. Sam lashes out with a rear foot, his eyes rolling. The father steps away in time, a finger pointing in accusation, then he clenches his fist as Sam backs himself down the metal plate and attempts to bolt. I'm holding his rope with all my strength. He's circling, whinnying, lurching, his whole frame full of mistrust.

"Lead him down the lane a little, Jodie. That'll calm him down," says Sue, arriving back in the yard on Kaloo. She dismounts, her face full of concern.

"Can't we just force him in?" asks the man, looking at his watch.

"You don't want a terrified horse in your trailer," Sue responds. "He could damage himself and the vehicle."

I'm walking Sam down through the yard, past the entrance gate, and into the lane. It's good to get him away from the commotion. He moves swiftly, his mouth teasing my loose bun, the way he does before I mount him and we set off on one of our adventures.

"I'm not riding you today, Sam," I tell him. Normally by now, he would be snatching at the patchy winter grass by the side of the lane. His instincts for fight or flight are on red alert. I want to leap on his back and gallop him to the ends of the earth. I feel helpless. I can't protect him. I can't explain why this is happening. I will just be one more useless human in his life's journey.

There are footsteps behind me. If this is Leila, telling me to drag Samphire back to the yard, I'm going to lose it.

"Jodie? Are you OK?" It's Mom. I've never been so

grateful to see her. I shake my head. My chest starts to convulse. "Hey," she says soothingly, holding me close. Samphire whinnies—it's a short burst of his song. I think he's guessed what is coming. He rests his nose on my shoulder.

"They're loud and impatient and he got frightened. I thought Leila would be kind but she put on an act when she visited last time. She's not right for him, Mom," I tell her, my voice a plea. But there's nothing Mom can do. The miracle I've hoped for hasn't arrived by helicopter the way Ed's did. And the trailer is being moved down to the lane. Sue and Rachel are on either side of me now. Sue is putting a hood over Sam's head. He is letting out the most ear-piercing cry I've ever heard from a horse.

Somehow, my feet are moving and I'm leading him up the dropped ramp into the narrow space, tethering him. I stand holding him, feeling the quiver of fear in his abdomen. I am solid, like a monument, like the Arc de Triomphe in Paris, massive and impregnable. They will have to get a crane to lift me away or dynamite to turn me to dust.

But seconds later I'm in the lane again and Mom has a hand around my waist and Rachel is beside me and the ramp is being secured. Leila is giving me a little wave and closing her passenger door in the dark Land Rover. I can see Sam's rump and his hooded head, and now they are receding, the sound of his back hooves lashing out against the metal sides and his frightened cry filling the icy air.

I feel hot and my vision is blurring, narrowing into a dark tunnel. I'm spinning inside it, thrown into the vortex, somersaulting at the speed of light. Nausea is rising from my belly. My whole body is sweating. I'm on my knees in the earth, the wetness of the soil soaking through my jodhpurs, its coldness burning.

And when the sound of Samphire in distress has become just an echo in my pounding brain, I am sick. Everything is black and distant and peaceful now. I never want to open my eyes again.

Chapter Twenty-Eight

"Don't come down till we call you, Jodie," calls Mom. I'm sitting on my bed, taking deep breaths and trying to calm myself for the challenge I'm about to face—phoning Leila. It doesn't help that I can hear low voices in the kitchen, some giggles and someone saying "Shhh."

Mom and Ed have been up to something for days. There have been secret phone calls, family conferences, and shopping trips to which I haven't been invited, exchanged looks, and odd questions, a bit like an interrogation. For example:

Ed: Aside from he-who-shall-not-be-named, what special thing would you really, really like in the *whole* world? Anything, from skiing off Mount Everest to surfing on molten lava?

Me: (yawning) Oh, I don't know. A chocolate factory.

Ed: (narrow eyes, making notes with his fluffy ostrich pen) Is that a visit or a whole one to yourself?

Mom has been behaving equally weirdly, talking about the flowers in the garden one minute and then asking whether I've spoken to Rachel lately or considered going to the stables or joining an after-school club, almost in the same breath. I think she hopes if she says it quickly, I won't get grumpy and stomp off.

It's true I have been a moody dudey, as Ed would say. After Samphire went away, I hit what our doctor says was a "bit of a wall" for a month. I was off school, off food, off life. All the tests I was sent for came back negative. The educational psychologist I was referred to concluded that the shock of selling my horse had reawakened the grief of losing Dad and this added to the stress and worry of Ed's illness. I was suffering from PTSD, post-traumatic stress disorder. It would pass. We had to be patient. I needed complete rest and a great big chill pill (Ed's suggestion).

School was OK about it. I started getting work sent home, just like Ed. He and I would sit at the kitchen table, playing catch-up and betting who could finish first. I think it was actually good for Ed to have the company. He's had a lot to deal with since the operation. There have been some blips—a couple of infections that had us really worried. But he's always so positive. "So far, so goody gum-drops," he keeps saying, and now his consultant agrees, which is the best news ever.

Mom flitted about, pretending to be busy when we both knew she was watching us like a hawk. I heard her crying on the phone one night. When I asked her about it the next day, she said she was talking to A.C. and that sometimes she gets lonely, even though we're here all the time.

Then something unexpected happened. Mom's old editor, Rubber Gloves, called to offer her a contract for regular features on a new gardening magazine, working from home. Mom said that once the work started, we would be able to manage very well, as R.G. had worked a minor miracle and payment for the work would be really good. So I decided to do two things. The first was to take the big step of going back to school. While Ed is busy with his planes, which is most of the time, Mom can concentrate on her writing, without me getting under her feet. It was weird getting on the bus again, but after just one day, it felt like the same old, same old. My teacher was lovely. She wrote "Welcome back, Jodie" in big letters on the whiteboard, and the Glossies told me they were going to buy me a manicure set, now that I was horseless, then changed their minds. It was a kind gesture, sort of, but Ed put it very succinctly.

"Duh."

I sat with Poppy on the way to school and she gave me an envelope. Inside was a CD she had put together for me—all her favorite tracks. I love all of them. It looks like we have exactly the same taste in music. I think we might become friends.

Rachel pops in at home sometimes and tells me the stable gossip, but I haven't been back there yet. Just thinking about the place makes me feel panicky. I hold the lock of Samphire's mane in my hand at night and in my dreams, we're riding together. Dad is usually with us and we're laughing in sunlight. It's horrible waking up and remembering the truth. My subconscious seems to have gotten stuck in the past, muddling my memories, taunting me. Sometimes I have nightmares. Samphire is tied up in a burning stall and although I'm there, I can't move to raise the alarm or rescue him. His screams make me cry out and Mom comes running. On those nights, I usually end up in her bed, on Dad's side, with my eyes wide open until the dawn starts to break.

So the second thing I decided to do was to make a call, which is why I have the phone in my hand. It's taken me a long time to work up the courage to call the number on the piece of paper I've kept in a drawer for the last five months. I've tried to run through the conversation I'm about to have and prepare myself for things not going too well. I'm not sure I'll cope if the news isn't positive. Whatever happens, I have to know what the situation is.

I count the rings and am up to twenty when a young female voice answers.

"Hi?" she says, a bit out of breath.

"Hi, is this Leila?" I ask. My voice is trembling slightly.

"Yeah. Who's this?"

"It's Jodie Palmer, Samphire's last owner. I was wondering how he's settled in with you."

"OK," Leila responds. I can hear something like indifference in her tone.

"That's good," I say. My mind is racing. *Just do it, Jodie.* "But I wanted to say my situation has changed and I'm serious about buying him back. If you wanted to sell him, I could give you two hundred more than you paid for him."

"Cool. Maybe. Yeah. I'm sort of over horses, especially crazy ones," she sighs. "My dad's been saying we should get rid of him before the winter." My heart leaps.

"Could I speak to him, please?" My heart is hammering in my chest. I might be just a conversation away from getting Samphire back.

"He's out, sorry," Leila answers.

"Could you pass my message on to him when he gets back? And ask him to call me?" I'm almost begging.

"Sure. What's your number again?"

I give her my home phone and my cell, and Mom's cell for good measure. Leila writes them all down, says, "OK, bye," and hangs up quite abruptly. There was so much more I wanted to ask. In what way has Sam been "crazy"? Has he thrown her or just been disobedient? Is he eating well or is he pining? But Leila obviously didn't want to discuss it. The important thing is, she may soon be ready to *sell him back to me!*

That's why I'm kissing the phone receiver and doing a little dance next to my bed.

For the first time in months, the knot in my stomach is loosening and a surge of energy flows through my body.

Now that Sam's return is a real possibility, I need to start saving big time. Mom said that, in a couple of months, she would be able to help with Sam's livery costs again. But I have to raise the lump sum for his purchase. I'll do it somehow. As soon as Mom and Ed say I can come downstairs, I'll tell them the good news.

Our family cloud suddenly has three silver linings: Ed's consultant says he can go back to school very soon; Mom's worry lines are disappearing now that she has a job offer...and I'm going to bring Samphire home where he belongs.

"OK, Jodie, we're ready!" calls Mom.

I'm running downstairs, two at a time. The kitchen door is closed and there is scuffling behind it. I turn the handle and push, waiting a moment before peeping around into the room. My eyes are met by banners and things going pop and helium balloons and quite a few familiar faces grinning at me.

There's Rachel and Sue, Mom and Ed, Rachel's mom and dad and, looking through the open back door, Rambo with a ribbon in his mane. He looks ridiculous, but cute. I'm wondering how they got him into the back garden when I notice a heap of presents on the table and all my favorite snacks on big plates near the stove.

"Surprise!" they all shout, letting off some more party poppers.

Seeing all of them and Rambo, a huge rush of emotions floods through my system; sadness, excitement, even a burst of happiness. If Dad and Samphire were here, it would be the best, best, brightest birthday ever. I hug them all in turn and Rambo most of all.

His mouth is exploring my pockets for slices of apple, and he nickers, disappointed, when he doesn't find any. I take a whole one from the fruit bowl and offer it to him. He whinnies in thanks and makes us all laugh.

"*Happy Birthday, Stick!*" yells Ed above the racket. It is already thanks to my family and friends. It's the perfect time to put Plan A—Rescuing Samphire—into action.

"Hi, everyone. Wow, thank you for all this. I don't know what to say, except…I have an announcement." And I tell them what I hope to do.

Rachel, who is always totally fantastic, immediately says, "How can I help?"

From today, a new phase of my life has begun. I'm on a mission. Look out, world. Jodie Palmer is coming back and she means business!

Chapter Twenty-Nine

"Come too," pleads Ed, nearly yanking my arm out of its socket. "It'll be fun at the beach, Stick." Piles of coins and dollars that I've been counting on my bed cascade into each other. *Erg, now I'll have to start again.*

"I can't. I've got homework and then I'm walking Snap, Crackle, and Pop," I tell him. These are the yappy terriers that live down the street. Their owner had a hip operation and needs help with their exercise, so I'm walking them regularly in my quest to save up. I also have a morning paper route, lead young kids on pony walks from the stables, and help out with yard duties. Rachel and I did a cake sale at the stables this week, which raised fifty dollars.

Mom's been fantastic as usual, and has given me a thousand dollars from her feature-writing money. I'm on track to raise the extra twelve hundred for Sam's purchase by the end of this month.

Leila's dad hasn't called yet. Mom says I should call him again when I've reached my target. And by then, she should be able to add some cash if necessary.

"I'll let you fly the Spitfire," Ed says. His computer-geek friend Leo is loitering just outside my door, probably picking his nose. Leo's mom has offered to take them out today.

"I'm sorry, Teddy," I say gently. "I need to work."

"How much do you have?" my brother asks, eyes wide at the sight of so many ten-dollar bills.

"About nine hundred. Just three hundred to go before I make that call."

"You're doing a good job, Stick," my brother says.

"Trying," I nod. "I'll get there. Have a good time, OK? And don't decapitate anyone, wing commander."

"Affirmative, squadron leader," replies Ed, saluting me.

"Bye, Leo," I call.

There's an odd shuffling sound and the clearing of a throat. "Yeah. Later," comes the shy, nasal grunt from the hallway.

I watch out of my window as Leo's mom reverses her car from our driveway into the lane. I can see the boys in the back, heads and hands moving like manic puppets, excited to the point of frenzy. I'm thinking how much Dad would have loved flying planes with Ed, sharing boy-time with him. Leo, who loves all things technical, is a good match for Teddy, though. It's funny how reading the spec of aircraft out loud passes for conversation between them. When they talk on the phone, it's like a code, full of numbers, followed by "Aaah, sweet."

The air coming through my window is full of summer scents. Birds are hopping around, pulling worms from the damp grass. I'm longing to be outside. Suddenly, my math prep seems less than appealing and I'm putting on my sneakers.

"Walking the dogs!" I call to Mom as I rush

through the hall downstairs. She's on the phone, doing research for her feature on gazebos.

"See you soon," she mouths at me, her hand over the receiver.

Moments later, I'm outside on my bike, pedaling furiously, lifting my legs in the air as my tires swish through the shallow puddles by the curbs. It's so great to be moving, breathing in the energy all around me. A warm wind whistles around my ears, whispering hope into my heart. It's a good start to Sunday, even if the hour to come will be full of terrier squabbles, muddy paws, and mini poo bags.

My hands are off the handlebars and I'm perched up on the saddle, hurtling down a small hill, which ends in a curve. Snap, Crackle, and Pop's cottage is about half a mile farther on. With luck, I might be able to freewheel some of it.

But just as I hit full speed, a glimpse of something white and large among the trees distracts me from my descent. I brake cautiously, aware that it's coming closer, keeping pace with me. Glancing sideways, I realize it's a stunning gray with an adult female rider, turned out in smart cross-country gear, traveling at full canter. She's urging the filly on with determination. They are keeping pace with me on the parallel forest track, navigating the mulch-covered pathway with precision. The horse looks like an experienced eventer and must be about seventeen hands—my heart is thundering in unison with its hooves, enthralled just by the sight of it, majestic in sunlight, a regal vision flashing intermittently between the lines of trees.

I slow the bike so that they will reach the bend before me and I'm rewarded with a full view as they cross the lane and set off on a new bridle path, which borders a stream. I watch impressed as they easily jump a large trunk obstructing the track. Two seconds later, they are gone, forging farther into the Forest, leaving me in awe, with a new ambition surging through my veins.

I'm going to ride like that someday, fast and

fleeting like an arrow, streams of mud flecks spattering from the hooves speeding on the wet terrain, the smell of fresh pine and fern bombarding my face. But I have a secret pact with Samphire, never to mount another horse until he's safely home. He and I will be reunited soon, I feel sure. And there will be a whole new world of challenges to explore together.

Was this a sign? A promise of things to come? I cross all my fingers at once to seal my wish.

Chapter Thirty

Darkness. Eyelids drooping, sleep creeping across my consciousness. A gray horse, galloping, riderless, in slow motion through shallow water; spray misting the mossy banks; the end of a rainbow, arcing through the droplets to the forest floor. I'm waiting, counting the splash of hooves. He's coming, mane flowing, ears forward, flank flexing with the easy strides. His gaze is focused. He doesn't see me, even though I wave and shout his name over and over. He thunders past, forcing me to leap for cover. When I look into his eyes, they are made of glass. There's a key buried deep in his side. Where it has been turned, blood trickles down his belly.

"Samphire!"

There is a gasp and a rattle near me. I snap awake

to find a figure near the end of my bed, fiddling with something on my desk.

"You gave me the heebie-jeebies, yelling like that," says Ed, accompanied by the chink of coins against glass.

"What are you doing?" I ask accusingly, clicking on my bedside light. Ed has his hand in my money jar. I wait for an explanation. Ed just shrugs, sheepishly. "If you needed to borrow money, Teddy, you should have asked."

"I don't," he replies.

"What?" I sigh. I look at my clock. It reads two a.m.

"Need to borrow money," he states.

"Your hand is still in my jar," I point out.

"There's a good explanation," he says with maturity.

"All ears," I tell him, plumping up my pillows and leaning back on them.

"Keep your voice down."

"Why?"

"Don't want Mom to wake up," he answers. "She doesn't know and she'll be mad, I think."

"What have you done, Teddy?" I whisper, my voice full of warning.

"I don't want to say," he replies.

"*What are you doing in my room at two a.m.?*" I demand.

"Shhhhh, Stick," he pleads, his finger to his mouth. The other hand seems to be stuck in the neck of the jar.

"I'm going to count to ten and then I'm calling Mom," I warn him. "One..."

"It's nothing bad," he tries to reassure me.

"Two."

"I just wanted to make things better."

"Three."

"Doh. It won't come out." Ed is trying to extricate his right hand.

"Four."

"OK. But I don't want you to be mad at me. Do you promise?"

"Five, six."

"That's not fair. You did two in a row," he complains.

"Seven."

"Ouch! There, it's out," Ed sighs, relieved.

"Eight."

"I think you're going to freak out. You weren't supposed to wake up and see it."

"Nine."

"OK," he says, "I sold the Spitfire and all my planes to Leo and he gave me two-hundred-and-fifty dollars so I was putting it in your jar and it was mostly bills but the coins were noisy, so there, smarty-pants, stuff that in your jodhpurs and sit on it." Ed's chest is heaving with this rapid-fire revelation. He is looking at me, waiting for a reaction. I know that my mouth is open, but nothing is coming out, even though "ten" is on the tip of my tongue.

"Why?" I ask, my brain struggling to catch up.

"You gave up Samphire for me. I can help you get him back," he answers with a shrug.

"But your planes..." I say. Ed's massive sacrifice is taking a while to sink in.

"They're for kids. I'll have a real one one day, like Dad," states Ed. He's trying to be manly, but that's hard when you're wearing Spider-Man pyjamas. "Are you mad at me, Stick?"

"Yeah. Really, really mad. Get in," I tell him, holding the duvet open. He grins from ear to ear and launches himself onto my bed.

"Can I stay till morning?" he asks.

"Yup," I answer, turning off my light. Ed is a terrible wiggler so this is a big gesture on my part.

"You're not going to give me a Chinese burn?" he adds suspiciously.

"Nope," I confirm.

"So, you're not mad at me?" He's poking my arm with his finger.

"Teddy, what you've done is the kindest thing ever. I don't know what to say, because thank you seems a bit lame, and not nearly enough," I tell him. "You are very special, little brother, and I think Mom will be really proud of you," I add, tousling his hair, but Ed is already asleep, or pretending to be, the corners of his mouth turned up in a smile.

Chapter Thirty-One

Today's the day. One-hundred-and-twelve paper-route miles, fifty-six dog-walking miles (times three), and forty-eight pony-leading miles since I started my fund-raising, I've reached my target. With everyone's help, I have raised enough money to buy Samphire back and pay a small sum toward his livery.

I'm pressing numbers on our phone and waiting for a ring. Mom and Ed are next to me on the sofa, gripping hands and holding their breath.

"It's ringing," I confirm.

"We know, we can hear it, Stick," shrieks Ed, unable to control his excitement.

"Yes?" answers a deep voice, slightly impatient. I recognize it as Leila's dad.

"Hi, can I speak to Leila please?" I ask, trying to sound confident.

"She's not here. Staying at a friend's. You can leave a message if you like," he says.

"It's Jodie Palmer. You bought Samphire from me," I explain. "Did Leila give you my message? I called a few weeks ago about buying him back. I wondered..."

"Yes?" comes the sharp response.

"Whether you've decided to sell him?"

"That horse was nothing but trouble from day one. Always trying to throw her. She lost interest so I sold him last month," responds Mr. Mackintyre, no trace of kindness, no regret in his tone. He sounds as if he's going to hang up. My head is suddenly throbbing with the rising pressure of blood in my veins.

"But Leila said she would call me!" I exclaim.

"That's not my problem," he says curtly.

"Please can you tell me who bought him?" I ask, panicked.

"Some bloke who paid cash. He went out of the county, that's all I remember. Glad to see the back of him. You had no business selling a horse in that state." The line goes dead, anger hanging in the air.

I'm staring at the receiver. Mom and Ed are looking at me in disbelief. I can feel my bottom lip trembling. Mom puts her arm around me.

"It's all been for nothing," I say, tears welling in my eyes. "Why didn't Leila call me?"

A wave of despair mixed with something vicious sweeps over me. I think it must be fury. It feels white-hot. I'm rigid, like stone. There are so many questions stabbing at my brain. Did Leila forget our conversation? Or worse, did she decide not to contact me out of spite? I should have called earlier, been more persistent. But maybe it wouldn't have done any good.

"It's all my fault," says Ed, running out of the room and up the stairs.

"It isn't, Teddy." I try to follow him, but my legs won't move.

"I'll go," says Mom. "You start thinking about Plan B."

"He could be anywhere." My spirit is shredded like a shot helium balloon.

"He could be horse meat," wails my brother's voice from the top of the stairs.

"Ed!" Mom exclaims.

"Sorry, Stick," he says. "Didn't mean to say that out loud."

I know that tracking Sam down will be almost impossible without an owner's name to go on, unless he becomes registered with the Pony Club or something like the National Show Jumping Association for events under his original title. But he could be called something different. The only way I'll find him will be by placing ads in papers and magazines with a photo, which will cost a lot of money, or scouring the country and looking in every stable and field.

It's a no-brainer. My hopes have hit a wall. Everyone's kindness, support, and generosity have been wasted. It's not true that sacrifice is rewarded.

"We'll think of a way," says Mom, after retrieving Ed from the landing. "The Palmers don't give up."

Mom's words ring in my ears as I ride my bike recklessly through the Forest, following a narrow track that weaves and winds its way between the oaks of the ancient woodland, ducking overhanging branches, swerving around deep, crusted ruts and roots.

I don't care about the uncomfortable vibration rattling my arms or the thin stems of foliage whipping my cheeks. Where the track forks, I take the worst-looking option, shrouded in bushes and obstacles, the path less traveled, and I push down on the pedals harder, faster, until pain screams in my calves.

When my luck runs out and my bike and I part company, I land with a thud, my face in foul-smelling leaf mould. My jeans are torn and blood seeps through the frayed cotton from a graze on my knee. I can taste the dankness of mushrooms and soil. My back wheel clicks as it spins to a stop, deformed by the impact with the stealthy stump, hiding under ivy.

I'm crying in big, desperate sobs, until I have no energy left.

I lie still, no will to get up. I feel like a fighter who has taken a massive punch. Shocked, winded, hurting, I've been backed into a corner. I'm on the ropes. Voices in my head are like a crowd, chanting for me to throw in the towel.

"Just give in, forget about him, get on with your life," they shriek.

But here on the forest floor, where there's nowhere farther to fall, something deep inside me is stirring. A fragment of defiance? The instinctive feeling that Samphire isn't far away? Perhaps a memory of Dad; something he said years before.

No decision is ever set in stone. There are always choices.

So do it, Jodie, my brain tells me. Get up. Brush yourself off. And while you're at it, why not get a few things out of your system?

For the next five minutes, I rampage around the small clearing, a large stick in my hand, thrashing at everything in sight. I'm yelling at the top of my voice, hammering with a fist on rough bark like an insane woodpecker, hanging by my arms from a bough, trying to wrench it from its source.

I drop back to the ground and stay hunched for a moment. The crack of twigs makes me look up. Ed is standing close-by. I can see his bike leaning on a tree. I wonder how long he's been there, watching me lose it.

"You OK?" he asks.

I shrug and stand up. "How did you know where to find me?"

"You always come here when you're mad." Ed grins and I find myself smiling back. I'm really pleased to see him.

"I got you M&M's." Ed holds out a purple packet of my favorite chocolates.

"Thanks, Teddy."

"It's true what Mom said, Stick," he tells me.

"Yeah, I know. We won't give up."

"Never," says Ed, making us put our fists together in a promise.

Chapter Thirty-Two

"No news?" asks Rachel, popping her head around the office door at the stables. I'm sitting at the desk, poring over all the latest magazines in the hope of spotting a photo or a mention of Samphire. I'm here more and more as the summer days turn into weeks, trying to keep the vision of him real in my memory. I imagine him back in the yard, grazing with Rambo in the field, giving me a hard time in the ring.

"Not yet," I respond, trying to sound bright. Everyone here has been so supportive. Sue even gave me some money to offer as a reward for information leading to positive identification. I've kept up my regime of fund-raising through the holidays and pleaded with Mom not to book us a trip so that I don't have to leave "Campaign HQ," as Ed calls home.

There were a couple of calls, which sent us scurrying

across state lines. Both led us to gray horses that resembled Samphire. One was a wounded steeplechaser who had been taken in by an equine charity. The other was an eight-year-old eventer who had been bought in Europe and shipped over. Our hopes came crashing down on both occasions.

Even Mom, who has never before shown signs of losing enthusiasm for my quest, is beginning to question the amount of time I spend emailing riding schools and pony clubs. She's mentioned it might be time to cut down on my part-time jobs and is concerned that my regular vigil at the stables is becoming a bit "obsessive." (I only slept in Rambo's stall once, but I can see her point.)

"It's like looking for a flake of snow in the Himalayas," Ed observed at breakfast. Since he's had his hair cut short for our imminent return to school, he's been coming out with quite profound things. He's also grown two inches during the summer. That must be a good sign. I don't like the fact that he's catching up to me on the height chart on the back of our kitchen door, though.

"Why don't you come with me for a hack?" asks Rachel. "It might be the last chance before school starts again." She pulls a face. At least she's going back as a ten-A-stars student.

For a moment, I'm tempted. The idea of a gentle ride through the leafy countryside, along woodland trails, stopping to let the horses drink from crystal clear streams, is very appealing. After so many weeks out of the saddle, I feel fragmented, as if I'm only firing on two out of three cylinders.

But a promise is a promise.

"No, thanks," I reply. "I'm going to head home soon. Ed's going camping and I want to be with Mom."

Ed's outdoor adventure is a first. Sleepovers in tents were never possible when he was having regular dialysis. The consultant is really pleased with him, which has made Ed grow in confidence and start doing normal kid things. I'm not sure camping with Leo and his dad, who is a vegan Hells Angel, counts as normal, but to each their own. I don't know what Ed will make of stewed vegetables for dinner. But after Mom's cooking, he should be able to cope with anything unusual.

"Jodie, are you going to stop riding forever if you don't find Samphire?" Rachel is voicing what everyone at the stables is thinking.

"I will find him," I state simply.

"But what if you can't buy him back?" she persists. It's a logical question, but my brain can't deal with any options other than the one I've set my heart on. Flexibility isn't one of my good points, I'm realizing.

"It probably sounds stupid, but I feel it's going to work out," I tell her.

And maybe it's just my imagination, but standing in the yard moments later, I can hear his song, so, so faintly, carried on the warm air currents of August.

"I'm not giving up, Sam," I say softly to the wind. It makes no reply, just carries my whispers away on an invisible journey.

Chapter Thirty-Three

"That's so cool, Teddy," I say. "I never knew there were grizzly bears in the Forest." Mom and I exchange glances and a grin. Ed is regaling us with his nighttime camping exploits, involving chasing away a huge, dark animal from the food supplies at three a.m. The three of us are sitting in Mom's bed in our pyjamas, having hot chocolate and cookies. It's after ten and the sky is a mixture of dusk and moonlight. "I saw its teeth—massive," breathes Ed, demonstrating a fierce bear face. "Leo's dad told us to bash the saucepans together to scare it off, but when it didn't move, he said we had to link arms and charge. Man, it was scary."

"Are you sure it wasn't a pony?" asks Mom.

"It was standing up on its back legs and it had a big

hairy belly," replies my brother earnestly. It sounds like Leo's dad, I'm thinking.

"Wow!" gasps Mom, a little too theatrically.

"You don't believe me, but you weren't there," states Ed huffily.

"It hasn't put you off camping then," she smiles, grabbing him for a hug.

"Nah. Didn't get a lot of sleep, though. There was all this barking and neighing in the night," he yawns. "Leo's dad really snored. And then some chickens started up before it got light. *Cock-a-doodle-doo!*" he screeches. "Crazy."

"What sort of neighing was it?" I ask. Force of habit.

"Mad. Like they were being attacked by wolves or something. But it was far away," Ed answers. "And it stopped in the morning."

"Maybe they were spooked by something," I suggest. Ed nods and yawns.

"Bedtime for adventurers," Mom says, looking at the clock.

"Can I sleep with you, Stick? Can I? Can I?" Ed asks. "In case the *bear* comes."

"OK. Then it can eat you first," I reply, pulling him out of Mom's bed by his arm.

"At least I'd be tasty, not sticky." Ed has gone limp like a rag doll. I'm using all my strength to drag him toward the door.

"Don't forget to brush your teeth," says Mom sleepily.

Ed and I go into the bathroom and jostle for the prime spot in front of the sink. Too much toothpaste gets squeezed onto our brushes so our mouths are soon full of white foam. Ed pulls monster faces in the mirror. Then he shrieks and squeals. His voice rises and descends like an opera singer performing while doing a bungee jump. The noise hurts my ears.

"Enough, stupid," I complain.

"Thas wha' vee'orses thounded like," he says, plumes of white liquid spurting from his mouth.

"Gross, Teddy," I moan, leaving him to it.

His impression has reminded me of something, though. I dismiss it from my mind, because it's late and I'm tired, so I'm probably imagining things. But it's a thought that won't go away, even when Ed has curled into a hamster ball next to me and is snoring softly, and the only sounds from the world outside are the hoots of distant owls in the Forest. The more I think about it, the racket Ed made wasn't just like an animal in fear or crying for help.

It was a horse's song.

Chapter Thirty-Four

"Can you show me where you were?" I ask Ed, as soon as he opens his eyes. I have an ordnance survey map of the Forest unfolded on my bed. Ed sits up, stretches, stares at the paper covering my duvet and hits his head.

"Sorry, Stick. Brain won't work without breakfast."

"Can't you just point to the area?" I encourage. Ed's index finger wags a no.

It takes twenty minutes and four homemade pancakes before Ed's brain is willing to work out where he stayed on his camping trip.

"It was really hilly," Ed tells me, reaching for his fifth pancake. I shake my head.

"Those are for Mom." Ed pulls a pained face. "Can't you remember the name of the place?"

"Nope. It was about half an hour from Leo's house," he replies.

"Which direction?" I ask, trying not to get irritated.

"Um. Right, I think." Ed licks the maple syrup off his plate.

"Teddy. This is important. Did you pass anything that could give us a clue? A school, a church, a bridge...?"

"We passed a pub called the Snail and Rocket. Or was it the Rail and Snocket?" Ed is creasing up with giggles. I throw my hands up in frustration. Mom comes in and kisses us both good morning.

"Mmmm. Pancakes," she says appreciatively.

"Or the Nail and Sprocket!" laughs Ed, holding his stomach. Mom sees that I'm starting to fume and gives Ed a cautionary glance.

"Sorry, Stick. I could show you."

"Show her what?" Mom's ears have pricked up.

"Where he camped," I reply before Ed has time to answer. "I was interested."

"You're up to something," says Mom.

"I wondered if we could go and take a look, that's all." I try to sound as if I'm not bothered either way. "It's an interesting place." That sounded a bit lame.

Mom's got a strange expression on her face. She knows I'm not into geography. "Maybe tomorrow if we get everything ready for school," she says.

My heart sinks. There's a long list of things to get ready for the new year, which will involve a trip for some new sneakers, a mouth guard, and backpacks for both of us. And tomorrow we're having lunch with Rachel and her family. It's our last two days of freedom. On Monday, we'll be back to the old routine.

"This doesn't have anything to do with horses by any chance?" Mom says at last, holding my gaze. It's no use pretending. She knows me too well. I nod.

"They were in distress—Ed said so," I say.

"Horses neigh for lots of reasons. I'm sure the owners dealt with it. I think you should put it out of your mind," Mom suggests, giving me a squeeze.

"How about I take you to the pizza place for lunch while we're shopping?"

"Ya ya ya!" is Ed's reply. I smile in agreement, but my thoughts from last night won't be quieted. Ed's story lifted the lid off a jack-in-the-box in my mind.

Chapter Thirty-Five

"This is a *bad* idea, Stick. You will be in so much trouble," whispers Ed. We jump as an owl at the bottom of our driveway hoots just above our heads.

"We'll both be in trouble, you mean," I say. I'm holding my mended bike still so that Ed can swing his leg over the back wheel. He sits himself on the metal frame and puts his arms round my waist.

I feel bad about involving him but I need him to show me where he heard the neighing. He's really excited and I keep having to tell him to whisper.

"Ready for takeoff, squadron leader," he instructs.

"Wilco, wing commander," I reply, pushing off with my left foot. Ed is humming the theme tune from *The Dam Busters*, one of Dad's favorite old movies.

In seconds, we're speeding down the lane, our

progress helped by the last light of the day. I'm hoping that Mom will stay absorbed in her feature work, content in the knowledge that she has said good night to both of us. As far as she's concerned, we're reading in bed. If we find the location without a hitch, we could be back within an hour and a half, according to my calculations. I've left the utility room window open, so we can sneak back in without her ever noticing.

It's risky, but I'm totally focused. Dad would never have abandoned a mission. I'm not turning back.

"Stick, slow down," complains Ed, poking me in the ribs. We've only been going for about ten minutes.

"Why?" I ask, keeping my eyes fixed on the lane and my feet pushing the pedals.

"Need a pee," he says sheepishly.

I pull the curb and Ed disappears behind a tree. I use the opportunity to check the map with my mini LED flashlight and flick on my bike lights. When Ed returns, I notice his pajamas showing under his jeans.

"What?" he says, embarrassed. "I forgot to take them off, OK?"

We set off again, using the back lanes to Leo's house and then following my plotted route through towns and across parks, past several families of grazing donkeys and forest ponies, to the Snail and Rocket pub, which lies about four miles from our house. From here, I'm relying on Ed's memory to get us to the location. We freewheel past at top speed, trying to avoid attention, noticing the string lights in the crowded garden and the noisy banter emanating from the open door.

"Up here," directs Ed, as we approach a turn, wobbling our way into it as he leans over too far, motorcycle style.

"Are you sure?" I ask him. The road is a single lane and there's an imposing metal gate with *Private Road* emblazoned on it just up ahead. The place looks like something out of a spooky film set with lines of tall fir trees disappearing into the thick gloom on either side of us. I shudder at their oppressive darkness and automatically check my cell phone for a signal. No bars. That's not a good sign.

"There's a path on the left," Ed says and we are soon faced with a neat stile and a reassuring wooden signpost. "We went up there, onto that hill. It used to be an Iron Age fort," he explains. "They sacrificed a lot of girls there. Kidding," he adds when he sees my less-than-amused face.

"I'll lock the bike up here," I say. "Are you sure this is the right place?" For some reason, there are shivers going up my spine. Maybe it's the dampness creeping up from the ground. That must be it. Nothing to do with all those stories about bad things happening to kids in the woods.

We walk and run, run and walk for about ten minutes, climbing the gentle ascent toward the stars. Eventually, Ed stops, turns in a circle and claps his hands.

"This is it," he confirms. "Look. Those are the ashes of our fire. And that's where I buried my cauliflower.

Yuck. Leo's dad eats it *raw*! Leo says he likes eating it but he doesn't really. Anyway, I dug the hole when they weren't looking. The peaches and brown sugar were nice, though."

"Teddy, that's great to know, but we didn't come here to search for vegetables." I'm casting my gaze down to the surrounding countryside. I can make out some fields beside the lane we cycled up where the tree line stops, some barns in the far distance, but nothing distinct. There are no lights anywhere, no sign of habitation. Everything is still and quiet, as if it's holding its breath. I strain my ears for any sound, even the faintest echo of a creature's call. Nothing.

"Where did the neighing come from, Teddy?" I ask.

"Mmm. That way. No, that way. Oh, I don't know. My ears can't remember. Can we go now, Stick?" asks Ed, hugging his arms round his body. An early autumn chill is wrapping us in a cold embrace. I give him a hug and rub his arms hard to make him warm again.

"Stick?"

"Shhh," I caution. "Listen." Ed pretends to turn to stone and holds a silly pose. He manages this for a whole minute. The landscape around us is still silent.

"I'm bored now," complains the statue. "And I'm getting nins and peedles. Aaaaaaah," he moans, hopping about on one foot.

Disappointment and growing feelings of guilt for asking Ed to come on this night adventure start to well up in my chest. Ed stops hopping and lays a small stone respectfully on the earth near the charcoal.

"Everything should have a grave. Bye, cauliflower," he says.

"OK, Teddy. Last one to the bike is a cabbage full of slugs." I set off at a jogging pace so that Ed can catch up.

"Hey, that's not fair. You started without me. Stick!"

We're running back down the hill, stumbling over the edges of rabbit holes. I don't mention to him that areas like this in the Forest are ancient burial sites and that we could be treading on the remains of long-rotten corpses.

This was a bad idea. What if Mom has discovered our empty beds? What if the police are scouring the countryside for us? Do you get a criminal record for wasting their time? The scale of the trouble we're going to be in is beginning to hit home, but something is niggling at the back of my mind. I don't want to give up yet, even though we should be heading back as fast as our legs can carry us.

"I think we should have a quick look up that private road, just to make sure," I say.

I grab Ed's hand to prevent him from falling and hurting himself as I pick up the pace and we keep running, filled with a new urgency. We reach the lane, retrieve the bike from behind a tree and fumble with the combination lock. Ed shines the flashlight on it and I click the four numbers into sequence. With a clunk, the clasp releases, like a snake uncoiling. I realize my hands are trembling as I wind it around my handlebars.

"Stick," says Ed in a hushed voice. He's pointing to the metal gate a little way ahead, which is now open. "It wasn't like that before." He gulps melodramatically.

"Come on, let's get moving," I whisper.

But we both freeze. Carried on the air, from the direction of the private road, the sound of frenzied barking and neighing suddenly assaults our ears. These are not animals spooked by the arrival of a fox in their yard. They are calling out in distress, in terror. And above the distant confusion of noise, one high-pitched call is so familiar, the hairs on the back of my neck stand rigid with fear.

Chapter Thirty-Six

I'm flying close to the ground, unaware of my feet working like pistons, turning my pedals. My eyes are almost blind with fury. Breath sears through my nose and into my chest. I drive it out in gasps. My hands grip the handlebars with all my strength, sending shock waves up my trembling arms.

No threat, no pain, no ordeal will dissuade me from reaching my destination. Never have I been so focused, never so sure of my instincts. Adrenaline is coursing through my body like liquid fire. If I yell, my voice will spew out red and orange flames.

The tarmac gives way to rough track with deep ruts, curving down into a valley. I'm descending into oblivion, into a dark place that holds a dreadful secret. Stones fly away from my tires, which skid over the fault lines in the caked mud and jam against the sides of grooves made by heavy vehicles.

Be quick, Ed. Raise the alarm. Tell them where I am.

I dropped Ed outside the Snail and Rocket only minutes ago with orders to get help. Now, I'm on my own, heading at full speed toward a horror I won't let myself imagine. The animals' cries are louder now, more anguished, guiding me toward them. And there are men's voices, raised in aggression, and the low rumble of an engine turning over, its exhaust blowing and rattling, adding to the commotion.

Ahead of me, I can make out a run-down yard with two dilapidated buildings, a barn, and a smaller store, now with its roof missing. In front of them, there's a large trailer and an old Land Rover, whose headlights are shining my way. It's the only source of light, revealing abandoned machinery rusting against a stone wall, iron skeletons dumped in a heap. I swerve my bike into the undergrowth, leaving it on its side, and continue on foot, hiding where I can, avoiding the bright beams.

Yelping, growling, shrieking, whining, snorting—the desperate alarms coming from what sounds like dozens of captive creatures is almost deafening.

What is going on here is not the work of a farmer giving his livestock a late feed. The place has a disused, clandestine feel. There are men moving furtively, not wanting to be seen. They open the back ramp of the trailer, which hits the concrete beneath it with a clang. Then one of them removes the wooden plank securing the barn doors and pushes. As he does so, the animals intensify their vocal protest and the barking from within turns to howling, more bloodcurdling than any wolves. Again the shriek of a single animal rises above the others, scaling several octaves, more like a call to battle than an expression of fear. A song I know by heart.

"Shut it, stupid horse," shouts the taller of the men who is the first to enter. "Get that rope around his neck, quickly. Load him first," he instructs his companion. There is an urgent sound of hooves kicking out against the corrugated wall of the barn.

I probably have about twenty seconds to disable the vehicle while they're not looking. A snap decision finds me silently opening the driver's door of the Land Rover and feeling for the keys. I've seen it done a hundred times before in the movies. But there's nothing hanging from the ignition.

"I'll show you—" yells the second man, and I hear the thud of something hard and unforgiving on flesh, followed by a scream and the clash of shoes against metal.

"He's broken my arm," I hear the man yelp, crying with pain.

"I'm gonna break his neck," comes the reply, together with a whole string of curses.

As I edge along the side of the trailer, I get my first glimpse inside the barn. The scene before me is more shocking than my worst nightmare. The countless silhouettes inside the stinking space tell me all I need to know. These poor animals are live cargo, destined for transportation. There must be a hundred emaciated dogs tied to upright beams, some guarding puppies, and maybe half as many horses and donkeys, tethered together so tightly there's no room to lie down.

There are also bodies strewn among piles of excrement, some so decomposed it's difficult to tell what type of animal they were. I do my best to stifle my reflex to be violently sick.

But above all this, rearing, bucking, lunging at his tormentor who is repeatedly bringing down a heavy wooden stick on his neck, there is a gray stallion as pale as death, his ribs prominent, his face a contorted mask of determination. His teeth are braced, and he is clearly fighting for his life, gathering the remnants of his spirit for a last assault.

I have to get him out of there this second, even though it means yelling and blowing my cover.

"*Samphire!*" I shout, but he doesn't hear me above the panic-stricken animals. If he runs now, I can save him. "*Samphire!*" I scream, waving my arms. The men turn to look at me, surprised, and the one giving the orders starts to move forward menacingly but wary of this great, gray adversary in his way.

Samphire, rising up on his rear legs, bellowing like a war horse, thrusts his front hooves toward the object of his hatred. He brings him down with all his force, making contact with the man's shoulder and knocking him to the ground.

The other man approaches from the side and tries to throw a halter rope over Sam's head, while his colleague writhes in pain.

"Got you, you raving monster," he snarls. Sam tries to step back and slip the rope off but there are other animals in the way, all shrieking with terror. The halter tightens. Sam rears and neighs, his eyes rolling.

"Now, boy, come now!" I call, but he buckles onto his knees, foam oozing from his mouth, sweat running down his face, the whites of his eyes bloodshot, all energy spent. As the man gets closer, ready to snare his prey more securely, I sprint forward and slip deftly onto my horse's back. He responds like a light brought to life with the flick of a switch, rising like a Phoenix from the ashes. With a shake of his head and a final kick, the halter flies off and Samphire leaps, with a noble groan, toward the freedom of the yard.

In a split second, we're cantering awkwardly up the track, the ridges of his bones rubbing my calves and thighs, the grunt from his throat telling me how much effort every step is taking. Bridleless, he uses every one of his senses to navigate his way, but every step seems to cause him discomfort, his weak legs stumbling on the uneven surface. We don't dare slow down. The only way to reach safety is to keep going as fast as possible. I urge him on, saying his name over and over. He's holding his head high, proud and undaunted, but his breaths are labored, rasping in his throat. He is running on willpower alone, this brave and beautiful stallion. And he's doing it for me, for the bond we have, for the promise I made him.

Far behind us, I can hear the revving of an engine

and the squeal of brakes as the Land Rover is turned around, ready for pursuit. If only I could have found those keys and thrown them in the bushes.

On we ride, to the top of the incline and toward the point where the track melds into tarmac. Sam's pace is slowing, despite my encouragement. One hoof is dragging and scraping—oh God, please don't stop now. The SUV is laboring up the track and is probably only a hundred yards away.

"Not much farther, Sam, good boy," I say, my voice disintegrating, my body aching from the effort of gripping on to Samphire's once magnificent frame.

I must stay positive. I try to imagine Sam and me on the beach, galloping through shallow surf, sunlit and serene. If I close my eyes, I see us both, but the image fades and darkens, like the shutter of a camera closing.

As we pass the open gate with the *Private Road* sign, Samphire's body starts to tremble like an earthquake, shuddering in waves. I should close the gate to slow our pursuers, but without reins Sam is making the decisions. Still he labors on along the dark corridor through the trees; it can only be another mile, I tell myself, straining to see ahead in the darkness.

But the Land Rover isn't far behind us. Its headlights have us in their glare. Pressing my right leg against Sam's belly and my hand against his neck, I ask him to swerve off the lane into the trees. He responds, sensing my rising panic. We must find or force a path through the woods in order to reach the pub. The tall, slim trunks are like soldiers, standing to attention. Their lines are long and ordered. There is just space for a horse between them. Trotting as fast as he is able, Sam's survival instinct guides us through the black maze.

"No barbed-wire fence," I repeat in my head, like a mantra. Such an obstacle would surely bring us down. We would be trapped, at the mercy of the animal traffickers. "Clever boy, Sam," I praise, stroking his lathered neck. "At the end of this, there will be the biggest bucket of mash you've ever seen."

We're in the thick of the forest, about fifty yards from the Land Rover, which is driving parallel with us. I'm not sure they can see us, but it feels like the men are waiting for us to falter so they can make their move. There is the faintest amber light filtering through the trees ahead. Maybe it's just a mirage in this dark desert, a trick of nature, luring us from our objective. Are we still traveling in the right direction? I feel confused and lost. And Samphire is treading more unsurely, his nostrils flared, smelling danger. He is slowing to a complete stop and, despite my frantic instructions to trot on, he stands still, every muscle taut, every nerve engaged.

For a moment, there is silence. My legs have turned to jelly. I'm holding my breath, trying to let Sam assess the situation. He is unsure and makes a grumbling noise in his throat, pawing at the earth with one foot.

And then I see them, maybe twenty yards away; beams of white lights, crisscrossing their way through the trees like luminous sabers. They must be coming after us with flashlights. There is no decision to make. It's pointless trying to hide a gray stallion behind narrow firs. We'll have to ride deeper into the forest and hope to stumble on an escape route.

"Let's go, Sam," I whisper, urging him with my legs. He moves in a circle, fretting, but won't obey. "Please, boy. Do this for me one more time," I implore. He sidesteps and lowers his neck. The trembling returns with full force. He makes a low moan, but then raises his head high and throws his weight into movement with a lurch that nearly dislodges me from his back.

He's half-trotting with jerky strides toward the lights and nothing I can do will persuade him to turn around. It must be a trap and we are stumbling right into it. I'm thinking of Mom and Ed, whom I might never see again; of the stables and the good friends I've made there; of Dad, who used to say he had a date in his diary to walk me down the aisle, one day in the future, and it would be his proudest duty ever.

Life doesn't always work out the way you think, does it, Dad?

The amber glow is clearer now and tells me that we're almost at the periphery of the woods. The beams have become circles, like wolves' eyes, looking directly at us, and I can make out the shape of people behind them, moving purposefully. I'm gripping Sam's neck and I can taste blood where my teeth are biting my lower lip.

Suddenly, Samphire drops onto his knees, his lungs emitting deep grunts as he tries to maintain his breathing. I dismount quickly, just as he rolls onto his side in the dew.

"Oh my God, I'm so sorry, Sam. You've brought us as far as you can, haven't you?" I'm crying now and, danger or no danger, I don't care anymore. My heart has ripped in two.

"Stop!" commands a deep voice a little way ahead. "Stay where you are."

A face comes into view, then another and another. I

can just make out uniforms and then stern expressions giving way to concern.

"Jodie Palmer?" asks a short female, who has a radio in her hand.

I gasp at the unexpected sound of a gentle, female voice. I kneel down next to Samphire as relief floods through my body.

"Yes. There are two men in a Land Rover, and they've been keeping animals in the barn up the lane. Trafficking them. I rescued Sam. They were chasing us..." I blurt out, stroking Samphire's neck, which is heaving in an attempt to raise itself. "He's hurt. He needs help." I'm sobbing now, unable to control myself, exhaustion mixing with hysteria in a liquid stream from my eyes and nose.

The woman is speaking into her radio handset, but I don't hear the words. My head pulses and my ears throb, as if I'm passing at top speed through a tunnel.

An instant later, a police siren blasts through the barrier of my deafness and the night is ablaze with the lights from half a dozen vehicles that are blocking the road ahead. There are more voices shouting and the officer in front of me says something else into her receiver. She tells me the two men have ditched the Land Rover and are running with police in hot pursuit. She says everything will be all right.

I'm trying to believe her but looking at the suffering animal at my side, I know justice comes at a terrible cost. It shouldn't be Samphire who pays the price.

Chapter Thirty-Seven

"Keep fighting, brave boy, and get well," I whisper in Samphire's ear, expecting it to twitch in recognition. He isn't responding. His lashes flicker over his half-closed eyes, which seem unmoving and far away. Lying in the straw of his old box stall at Whitehawk Farm Stables, the full extent of his starvation is clear. His chest looks shrunken, the skin on his flanks is like thin cotton over fine china. His mane and tail are matted and gray with dirt. There is so much bruising across his neck where the wooden weapon came down that it has swollen up like a tire.

We needed a sling and a team of helpers to load him into Sue's trailer in the early hours of this morning. The vet, Greg Thomas, says it's a miracle that no bones are broken. He's warned me that Sam is so weak his heart may not be strong enough to help him through recovery, but he's given him a combination of painkillers and drugs to treat the infection in his lungs and put him on a drip to keep him hydrated. The next twenty-four hours will be critical.

We're keeping a vigil by his side, Mom, Ed and I. Mom is as white as a sheet from all the worry—and from telling me off. It turns out she called Leo's dad and the police even before Ed raised the alarm, having discovered we were missing at about ten thirty. She guessed where we had gone and was on her way to meet Leo's dad and follow him to the campsite. Ed said she went off like a firework when he told her that I'd gone back alone.

Samphire was calling me. What else could I have done?

There will be time for explanations and apologies. For now, Ed is leaning against Mom, covered by a horse blanket, fast asleep. Mom is watching me, like a guardian angel, and I'm resting my hand on Samphire so that he knows I'm here and that I will never leave him again.

He's one of the lucky ones. The police say that five of the horses in the barn were dead and two had to be put down on the spot. The same fate befell many of the dogs. Only the very toughest have survived after days with no food. Out of a total of eighty animals, only forty-five were saved. Several local animal charities have rallied and are collecting the survivors. All will be cared for and as many as possible returned to their owners or found new homes.

That's the good news.

The police also say that the creatures were probably stolen from across the region, often to order, by a gang. The plan had been to drive them to auctions in other parts of the country and the money raised would be used to import drugs through a network reaching as far as China. It seems that something had gone wrong, the plan changed and the animals were abandoned, until the two men turned up with orders to move some of the horses. At least now the pair are in custody.

"It's a big trade," the officer explained to us. "When the thefts are sporadic, it's hard to find a pattern. Holding areas are always tucked away in the country-side, so unless a member of the public notices or hears something suspicious, it's unlikely that we'll locate them. Hopefully, this is one gang that will never be able to lay hands on another animal."

Mom said that despite our reckless actions, Ed and I had saved a lot of lives. I think it was her way of saying we're forgiven, as long as we never, ever take off without telling her again.

"It's almost morning," she comments now, indicating the lightening sky beyond the stable door. My vision is blurred with tiredness. To me it looks like the blank screen of a TV that has been left on standby. I'm aware that horses in neighboring stalls are beginning to stir. There is the odd stamping of a hoof and a few snorts. Maybe Sam's friends are sensing his return and letting him know that they have joined our vigil.

The smell of the warm straw is luring my head down next to Sam's. I stroke his velvet nose gently, feeling the rhythm of his breathing, which is slow and weak. I touch his brow lightly and, with a sweeping movement, try to wipe away the memories of the terrible events of recent months.

"You're home, boy. That's all that matters now," I tell him before letting my eyelids droop and waiting for the welcome rush of darkness to envelop me.

"Stick. Wake up. Breakfast time," says a familiar voice, somewhere in the background of my dream about climbing the tallest tree in the world. The smell of bacon is wafting into my nose, and there are strong hints of fresh bread and tomato sauce, closely followed by hay and horse.

My eyes snap open and my brain reprograms itself to reality. There is no tree. But there is a toasted sandwich on a plate about six inches from my mouth. Six inches in the other direction there is Samphire, who is lying still on his side in a drug-induced sleep. Flashbacks batter my brain as I sit up, rubbing my aching neck. I am almost dizzy with the images of animals in distress.

"Mom says you have to eat," says Ed, who is sitting in front of me, legs crossed, staring at me like I'm an exhibit in a museum. But the fried meat smeared in red gloss has lost its appeal.

"Hot chocolate would be good," I say.

"Wilco," replies Ed, hurrying out of the stable, his protruding pyjama bottoms dragging on the ground.

It's eight a.m. I've slept for about four hours. While the world outside goes about its business, the yard bustling with the activity of Sue's weekend team tending to the horses, I begin an inspection of my stablemate, making a mental note of any positive signs of change. The swelling on his neck has reduced a little. There are sores on the underside of his belly I hadn't noticed before. Daylight also reveals that the rims of his eyes are red and raw, a sign of infection.

His eyes are half open. What's that in his pupil? A reaction? An attempt to focus? I look closely. It's like gazing into a deep, deep well, devoid of life. The valiant stallion from last night has been diluted away by the strong drugs. I hope he's lost in good dreams. I can't bear to think of his confused mind wandering in darkness.

I run my hand along his neck several times, dispersing clusters of mud. His mane is matted, with clumps of hair twisted into each other. It will take hours to tease them out, wash them, and brush them back to their former glory. I hope with all my heart that I will get the chance to cleanse away all the dirt from his awful experience. I want to groom him until he shines.

"Sorry, Stick, I tripped over a brush and the froth fell off," says Ed, appearing with a steaming hot chocolate straight from the stable kitchen. He passes it to me carefully, the handle toward me, then shakes his fingers like a lunatic as he's a complete baby when it comes to hot things. Like all the mugs here, this one has a cute pony on it and chips on the rim.

"Thanks, Teddy. Did you put some extra sugar in it?" I ask, taking a sip.

"Aaargh!" he answers, hitting his head with his hand. "I forgot. Don't you have any lumps in your pocket?" This assumption makes me smile. I shake my head, which makes me realize how stiff my neck is.

"It's fine," I tell him. "Where's Mom?"

"Talking to a reporter and another dude with a camera. It's you they want, but Mom said no," Ed answers. He leans toward me and confides in my ear. "I think that's silly because we could have gotten *lots* of money."

"I don't want to speak to anyone, Teddy," I tell him, relieved that Mom is defending our privacy. Ed nods, a little disappointed. I think he's probably confusing the local press with *People* magazine.

"Mom's brought us some clothes from home," he informs me. "I can sit right here while you change out of those smelly things and if he moves a muscle, I'll call you," promises my brother, keen to help. He produces his cell phone and waves it in my face as proof. I glance down at my filthy sweat pants and hoodie and have to agree that a shower and some clean clothes would be a good idea.

"OK, but if he so much as twitches . . ." I say.

"Yup. Understood," responds Ed, sitting down in the exact spot where I've made a dent in the straw. "Hey, Stick?"

"What?" I answer, on the alert.

"If you don't want your sandwich, can I have it?"

"Yeah, go ahead." I suppose on the scale of things a little tomato sauce won't hurt him.

"Oh my God, *Stick*!" he says, almost breathless, leaning over Sam.

"What is it, Teddy?" I answer, by his side in a flash.

"Didn't know horses got boogers," Ed observes, examining Sam's nostrils from every angle. "Gross!"

* * *

It's five p.m. Greg the vet is here again, very concerned that Samphire hasn't made any attempt to move. He takes his temperature and finds that Sam is running a fever. His neck and shoulders are breaking out in a sweat. Greg gives him an injection and fixes up another bag of saline, which will drip through a plastic tube into Sam's leg vein. It's vital to keep him hydrated.

"Poor guy," sighs Greg. "He's gone through the wars. He's a fighter, though, Jodie. No doubt about it."

"World champ," I answer, although my voice sounds a little hollow.

Greg gives me a warm smile and a squeeze on my shoulder and says he'll be back in the morning, unless we need him urgently before that. I imagine him going home to his family, reading bedtime stories to Lulu and Sunny, his three-year-old twins. He says they don't sleep and that's why he looks so bug-eyed. I think the truth is he's had a horrible time as the vet in charge of putting down the sick animals from the barn.

"How's it going?" asks Rachel, appearing in the space above the stable door. She pops her head in every hour or so to see if we need anything. She also reports back to Sue and the others to save us from being bothered by too many visitors.

"Not so good," I reply. "He's got a fever."

"I brought someone to see him," she says. "Come here, trouble."

I hear the scraping of big hooves and, seconds later, the large, friendly head of Rambo looms into the stall, nose outstretched and sniffing the air intently. He seems pleased to see his old friend, but perplexed too. He murmurs and mutters, a deep, gravelly sound coming from his throat. All of this is followed by a whinny, which bounces around the wooden walls, as shrill as wind chimes in a strong wind.

"Thank you, Rambo," I tell him. "Whatever it was you said, I'm sure it was very nice."

"OK, visiting time's up," says Rachel, reaching in to take hold of his halter so she can lead him away. At first he's resistant, avoiding her grasp. "He hasn't eaten his breakfast this morning," she tells me. "I think he's having his own vigil."

"Maybe he can come back later and check on Sam's progress."

"Yeah, if he's good," agrees Rachel, while Rambo rubs his face up and down her arm endearingly.

A nice policewoman called Jane comes to take a statement from Ed and me and the process lasts about half an hour. I have to describe exactly what I saw and the order things happened in. I get very upset at the point when I recall seeing Samphire through the open barn doors and realizing the danger he was in.

How many times did the man hit him, she keeps asking. Two, three, four? I replay the scene in my head with my eyes closed. Mom puts her arm around me when she sees I'm trembling. I answer the questions as accurately as I can. Part of me can't believe that this is real. Jane says it's a normal reaction and that I'm probably in shock. Ed likes describing how he ran into the pub's bar and demanded the landlord call the police.

"I told him there was no time to lose and that my sister needed immediate backup," says Ed very seriously. I see Mom and Jane exchanging a smile at this.

"You did exactly the right thing, Ed," confirms Jane. Ed beams, as if he's been given ten gold stars.

Afternoon morphs into evening. Mom and Ed return with a pillow and sleeping bag for me, plus some yummy pizza, salad, garlic bread, and strawberries. Sue said she'll stay with me after eleven tonight so that they can get some proper sleep.

I'm busy sponging Sam's body with cool water, trying to ease his fever, which seems to be getting worse, not better. I keep talking to him, telling him he's the best horse in the world, sometimes just spouting gibberish about anything from not wanting to go back to school to Snap, Crackle, and Pop and what a pain they are when they decide to go crazy, get their leads in a tangle around a tree, and start a group yapping thing.

He doesn't respond. Occasionally, a leg will twitch as if he's trying to unsettle a fly. One even kicked out earlier, but I think it was a muscle spasm and not a conscious action. His mouth is slightly ajar and I'm dripping mineral water from my bottle onto his tongue, which looks like a sick whale marooned on the ocean floor.

Eleven thirty p.m. and I'm starting to panic. Samphire is really agitated, although still in a semi-unconscious state. All his limbs are moving and his head keeps jerking up and down in the straw. It's as if he's trying to run from something and, in his flight, he's managed to dislodge the drip from his leg, which means he's not getting any pain relief or hydration.

Every so often, a mournful cry seems to erupt from deep in his belly. Is he moaning in pain? I feel he's trying to communicate, but I don't understand. Touching him seems to offer no comfort. In fact, he's thrashing around so much that it's not safe to stay next to him. I move to the side of the stall, where I sit with my back against the wall, watching helplessly while Samphire confronts the demons of his illness.

Sue is on the phone to Greg, asking for advice. She's pacing in the yard, unsettling some of the stabled horses who are moving around in their stalls, disturbed by the break in routine.

After a couple of minutes, she leans on the stable door to give me an update. "Greg's been called out to a mare in foal on the other side of the Forest," Sue explains. "He doesn't know what time he can get here, so he told me what to do with this." She holds up a syringe full of clear liquid. "He left it here as a precaution. It's a tranquilizer and it will keep Sam calm. I'll need you to help me, Jodie. We have to try and keep him still while I put the needle in his neck."

"Okeydokey," I reply nervously. I'm looking at my horse, who is working himself up into a frenzy, with lather at the sides of his mouth—I wonder if attempts to subdue him are too late. Sue approaches cautiously, closing the stable door behind her. She motions for me to hold Sam's head down on the straw. It takes my full weight to achieve this. He writhes and seems to bare his teeth at me.

"Hurry, Sue," I say to her. She is feeling for the right place and her fingers are measuring a triangular point between his mane and shoulder blade.

"If I go too close to his spinal column, there could be nerve damage," she says almost to herself. "I have to find the space between that, the ligament and shoulder blade, which…is…here." She inserts the needle, checks there is no blood oozing, then attaches the syringe and presses its contents into Sam's muscle. For a moment, his resistance starts to ebb away. The agitation doesn't stop, though. He seems to want to stand and his legs are flailing, trying to get a grip. I don't dare let go of my hold on his head. Surely the drug will kick in and give him some peace?

"Greg said the dose was enough to bring an elephant

down," says Sue, shaking her head. "I think you should come out of the stall." She beckons me toward the door. She must think he is in his death throes from the expression on her face.

There are always choices…

"I'm not leaving him," I tell her, something beyond panic in my throat. I'm flooded with an emotion that has overwhelmed me once before, one so powerful it allows you to keep functioning in the face of the worst kind of disaster, although all your senses are numb. It goes beyond sadness and anger to the core of every cell of your being, probably right to your DNA, which is altered forever. When we lost Dad, I remember Ed saying he thought it had turned him the wrong color inside.

It's called grief and at this moment, it is filling me with such resolution that I could stop the world turning on its axis. If I let go of Samphire now, he could injure himself so seriously no treatment would be able to save him. Maybe he's had a bad reaction to the medication. Maybe his symptoms are already beyond help. But if I have to stay in this position all night, I will. And if it is his time to die and by holding him, it makes it less terrible and frightening, I'll do that too.

Chapter Thirty-Eight

"Huh? Ugh! Hey!" I say, half in the confusion of sleep. Something is tickling my neck and ears. I'm expecting to hear Ed giggling as he has been known to commit the early morning feather torture routine on several occasions. I reach out to pull my duvet over my head and escape his cruel game. My hand feels only the harsh texture of dried vegetation. My nose tells me that it is up close and personal with something very musty and not the vanilla scented pillow that is my normal night-time comfort.

I'm not at home. I'm in Samphire's stall. Memories from the night before flood back into my mind.

The last thing I remember seeing is dawn light through the open stable door. I must have crashed next to Samphire, exhausted by hours of soothing his poor, agitated body. There doesn't seem to be any movement next to me. I'm dreading opening my eyes. Close to me, I can hear a deep inhalation and exhalation. Is it my breathing? I roll on to my back, rub my aching eyes, and open them.

The vision that greets me is so unexpected, so amazing, so awe-inspiring I gasp and let both hands fly to my open mouth. Just a few inches away, there is a horse's face, staring at my own, nostrils moving like antennae. The deep, dark eyes are fully focused, the ears forward in anticipation. I reach up and stroke the soft, scarred muzzle, a smile as wide as a new moon spreading over my face.

"Hey, Sam," I whisper. I am at a loss for more words, gazing up at the creature standing above me, his neck arching down, his tail swishing the way it does before I saddle him up for a ride. I sit up and just put my arms round him, covering his face in a thousand kisses, relief and joy converging. He nuzzles me again, telling me he's had enough smooching, and then regales me with a long and melodic whinny, punctuated with several snorts and the pulling of funny faces. It's his song, the special music that first opened my heart to him—that echoed and drew me to him when he was lost. And the unique means by which he seems to be saying "thank you."

"You're welcome, Samphire," I tell him and bow my head to him in respect. Anyone watching would think I had lost my marbles. "Can I get up now, please?"

I lean on his front legs a little to make him back away. He takes a shaky step in reverse and tosses his ragged mane, telling me he needs attention.

"Me, me, me," I say to him. But my eyes are focused on his sagging hindquarters and his trembling front legs. Despite his frailty, he is holding my gaze, his eyes bright with expectation.

"Do you want some breakfast?" I ask him. He nickers and swishes his tail. "I'm taking that as a yes."

When I glance out of the stable, the yard is peaceful. It's early morning; probably about seven.

Birds are pecking around on the ground, picking up oats and seeds. Horses heads hang lazily over stall doors. Mist trails low across the adjacent fields and sweeps over the concrete road leading to the lane. From that direction, I hear footsteps. Sue and Greg come into view, talking earnestly and walking with haste. Greg is carrying his black case and looks as if he expects the worst.

"Guess what?" I ask. I take in Greg's larger-than-usual bug-eyes and realize he has been working all night.

I motion for Sam to come and stand next to me. As he stretches his head over the stable door, Greg unleashes a string of exclamations and nearly drops his bag. Sue, who is usually really grounded, gives Greg a huge hug and then does a little dance on the spot.

"You absolute star," says Greg, stroking Sam's face and tugging his forelock affectionately. "You too, Jodie," he adds, beaming at me. "You're quite a team."

"We're working on it, aren't we, Sam?" I reply. "Told you he was world champ."

"He may be up, but he's not out of the woods yet," Greg warns me gently.

"I know, but he'll get there, won't you, Sam?" I reply.

While Greg gives Sam a complete examination, I press the keys on my cell phone excitedly. There are two people who deserve to hear this latest news more than any others.

"Teddy? It's me. Are you in Mom's bed? That's great, 'cause I want you both to hear this." I'm holding the receiver to Samphire's mouth. "Say hello, Sam," I tell him. He responds with a low, throaty neigh. "Did you hear that?" I ask my brother. *Sam's standing up by himself!*"

"Told you," replies Ed calmly. Then I can hear Mom telling him not to bounce up and down, because something will break. Seconds later, I hear ecstatic screams coming from both of them, the kind you get at the fair when people are thrown upside down.

"Mom? I know it's a strange question, but are you bouncing on the bed too?" I say into the receiver.

Chapter Thirty-Nine

I feel sick. I don't have butterflies in my belly, but a small monster, gnawing with very sharp teeth. I raise my foot up into the shining stirrup and swing myself deftly into the gleaming jumping saddle.

"Break a leg," says Mom. That's what you say to actors before they go on stage, but it's not quite so lucky for riders, I'm thinking.

"Stick, just in case," says Ed, thrusting a piece of paper with a shape drawn in pen on it. "It's the map of the course." I don't have the heart to tell him it looks like a carrot and that I won't have time to consult a map on the way around anyway. I put it into the pocket of my navy jacket.

"Smile!" Mom requests, aiming her pink digital camera in my direction. I definitely have my eyes closed when the flash goes off. "You both look lovely," she beams.

I hope so, after getting up at five this morning to groom Samphire to within an inch of his life. Then there was the stress with my bun (Ed has ten thumbs when it comes to sticking pins in the right places), not to mention the TLC lavished on Sam's new tack and my boots.

It's been a major operation, nurturing Sam back to health, building up his strength and confidence and preparing him for a cross-country event—hours and hours of work and massive help from Sue, Rachel, and the girls at the stables, plus lots of support from Mom and Ed. Even Poppy has been lending a hand, dropping by to keep me supplied with chocolate bars for energy! All our efforts have been worthwhile because Sam looks completely stunning.

With the help of a reward given by some of the owners reunited with their lost animals and the money I raised to buy Sam back, I've been able to fit us both in some cool gear and pay for a whole year's livery. The extra time I've gained by not having to walk so many mutts and deliver papers has been spent on schooling Sam and getting him to event level.

It's been six months since he was clinging to life by a thread. Today, we're both here in the grounds of Lynton Manor, looking immaculate, not a hair out of place, ready to take part in the Forest's most prestigious cross-country race. Sam is turning heads wherever we go. He's so white he is almost luminous.

"Ith that Pegathuth?" asks a little boy of about six, who is standing behind the ropes next to us.

"His name's Samphire," I reply.

"Where are hith wings?" The boy is searching Sam's belly for signs of folded feathers.

The loudspeaker booms out: "Will competitors make their way to the waiting area please."

There are thirty of us taking part today—and we're all winners of qualifying events over the last month. Usually, races like today's have staggered start times and the horse and rider who finish fastest with fewest faults claim the prize. But Mr. Lynton, the owner of the manor, is a racing man and makes his own rules. We all set off together and may the best horse win.

"We're on, boy," I say, shortening my polished reins, giving Mom and Ed a little wave as we start to move forward. The twenty-two jumps, a mixture of gates and log stacks, are set at no more than three feet high, which Sam can manage easily. He's not used to racing against other horses, though, and the noise of cheering and clapping from the excited crowd is making him frisky and nervous.

Looking around, I'm the youngest rider by about three years. Samphire is the most inexperienced horse too, so it will be a test of courage and ability for us both. I hope I don't let him down.

Mr. Lynton, a man of about sixty with a mass of unruly white hair, stands on a decorated podium ready to start the race. Samphire makes a nickering sound.

He's eager to get going and I have to turn him in a circle to keep him calm.

I'm going through the course in my mind, having walked it with the other competitors yesterday, and I know where it might be possible to gain some seconds. My biggest worry is jump twenty, the pile of logs with the steep drop and wide stream on the other side. The landing is awkward and it would be easy to stumble.

There's no time to worry about that now. A race official is lining us up. Mr. Lynton is holding a hunting bugle to his lips. *BARARP!* We're off!

There's a huge cheer from Sam's fan club from the stables as we set off at a fast canter across the wide meadows that border the manicured lawns. The grass is tall and dry after weeks of no rain and the ground feels firm. I don't even have to urge Sam on. His ears are forward, his neck extended and he is keeping pace with the group of front-runners.

We're heading toward our first challenge, a wooden

gate with four bars. Eight horses jump before we do and the rest of the field is on our tail.

Three, two, one, *fold*, my inner voice tells me and I bend forward over Sam's neck as he tucks his front hooves under and launches us into the air. We clear the top with room to spare and land well, ready to speed away. Sam is responding so intelligently; it's as if he can read my mind. The slightest movement of my hand on the reins changes his direction and a gentle squeeze from my calf alters his speed.

So far, the course isn't daunting him. We're holding our position as we navigate through empty sheep pens, jump a log stack, and canter down a slope with grass-covered obstacles at the bottom. The horse in front balks at the sight of a whirling scarecrow and veers to our left. Sam has no such worries and weaves nimbly between log poles before leaping the series of cattle troughs.

Ahead of us is a straight, stony track with tall cornstalks growing on either side of it. I sense Sam shift up a gear. In moments, we are galloping neck-and-neck with a roan mare that seems to be laboring under the weight of a heavy male rider. He's using his whip and kicking her belly, poor thing. We nudge past her as the next challenge comes into view—some hay bales on top of a wide cattle grid.

"Steady, Sam," I say. He needs no encouragement. The Arabian stallion in him takes over and propels us forward. He jumps too soon, but the leap is so huge, it feels as if we're flying. Sam's feet hardly touch the ground before we're speeding at a gallop toward the woods, about twenty yards behind the leaders.

I shiver as we enter the cool shade of the trees. Sam senses this and his stride falters for a second. We're both remembering another time, just months ago, when we were running for our lives on narrow paths between trees, and every step seemed like it could be Sam's last.

But today, his courage is matched by his strength.

He must look like a bolt of white lightning streaking through the dappled shade. *Maybe his mane is full of fairy dust, eh, Dad?* The thought makes me smile.

One by one, we tackle the jumps laid out along the route through the Forest. Some have flags and wind chimes hanging nearby to add distraction and to test our mettle. One even has posters of bears on it. (Ed would love it!) Mr. Lynton promised us a few surprises on the way!

There's another gray close at our heels, but we lose him after he refuses the three parallel stacks. I hear his rider arguing with the race official who has disqualified him. It won't do any good. The rules of the day were very clear. One hesitation and you're out.

I'm staying low over Samphire's neck, trying to make us as aerodynamic as possible. Every so often, I glimpse a glint of horseshoes in the shafts of sunlight ahead. The thud of hooves is reverberating through the trees, pounding through my body. I'm sweating and my vision is starting to blur.

"Come on, Jodie, you're doing fine," encourages a voice in my head. I could swear it's Dad's...

I can see bright daylight now beyond the line of beeches—the front-runners are spreading out into the open ground. We're not far behind them and, with just three jumps to go, I'm daring to think that we might make an attempt for third place. Ed and I have already discussed what we would do with the prize— two-hundred-and-fifty dollars. We were having one of those "In your dreams, if you were rich, what would you buy?" conversations. We decided Mom should have a special present, like a spa break or a trip to see some beautiful gardens in France or Italy, and agreed we would save up for this in any case. Neither of us expected Sam and I to have a real chance of making the top three.

Imagining Mom's happy face as we present her with the prize makes me urge Sam on even faster. He responds willingly. I notice his neck is damp with exertion. I relax the reins a little, not wanting to push him beyond his limits, but he just thrusts his head out and gallops flat out.

I glance back. The next competitor is quite a long way behind us. I can afford to focus fully on the leaders—a black gelding and a chestnut hunter. The gelding looks like a tank on legs, almost unstoppable, but the hunter is on his tail. There's a piebald and a bay behind them, side by side. Sam and I will need a huge helping of luck to get past them.

We stay very close them, and as we approach a bench jump, they diverge and create space and Sam claims it as his own. We take the jump just after the bay and the piebald is forced to hold back. Now Sam is neck and neck with the piebald, which is grunting with the effort of the fast pace.

The finish line is in sight, about a hundred yards away, and spectators are lining the route. There's a lot of noise and applause, but I can hear someone shouting "Go on, Sam, go on, Jodie." It's Rachel. She must have run all the way to the end of the course to cheer us on.

There are still two jumps before the final gallop to the finish. As we approach the huge grass mound with the steep drop to a stream, I try to steady Sam's head, but he's having none of it. We're moving past the piebald and gaining ground on the hunter.

Flecks of foam flick onto us from the chestnut's mouth. She's giving it all she has. We are almost level with her shoulder. The jump is wide and we take it together, landing on the top of the bank, leaping down over the stream. The hunter stumbles as she lands, giving us a fraction of a second's lead. Sam accelerates away like a lightning bolt.

Incredibly, we're in second place. Ahead of us, the black giant is lining up for the last jump, the gates laid out in a V-shape. The angle for takeoff is really tricky. I paced it out on my walk-through, but now I can't remember. Was it better from the left or the right?

"Come *on*, Fosca," the gelding's rider is shouting. Tension is so high now, I feel Sam shudder at the sound of her voice.

"Just one more, boy," I say to him. The crowd is roaring on our left.

Fosca's long stride is putting distance between us as we descend a gentle slope leading to the gates. It's a good thing he is ahead on this stretch. I'll be able to see which part of the jump he's going to leap. We need to give him space, or the result could be catastrophic—a midair collision.

As Fosca heads toward the right gate, I guide Sam to the left, giving the dangerous V-shape a wide berth. I expect to see the huge black frame airborne any second, but Fosca suddenly balks at the sight of the structure and veers across our path, taking off over the left gate. Sam swerves and I'm flung out of the saddle. My right knee is still hooked over the pommel and I manage to haul myself back into a seated position just as Sam makes a decision and launches us into the air.

We soar over the sharp apex of the gates, stirrups flapping, and make a secure landing. Fosca must be about five seconds ahead of us. His head is stretched out and he's galloping as if his life depends on it.

"*Go on!*" yells his rider, using her crop on his glistening flank.

"*Go, Sam, Go!*" I respond, willing my beautiful, brave horse to give our adversaries a run for their money. Sam needs no incentive. Ahead of him lies a flat stretch of ground. He knows what to do. It's in his genes. I grip my knees tight into the saddle. My feet locate my stirrups, but I don't kick back. I don't need to.

Fosca is listing to the right, his gait unsettled by his near-refusal. It gives us a chance to ease forward, to race shoulder to shoulder with the dark colossus, whose eyes are white-rimmed with exertion.

The line is a few yards away, we are behind Fosca by a nose. My eyes are fixed on the ribbon ahead, my body is low over Sam's neck. The noise from the crowd is a wall of sound. As if in response to it, Sam almost leaps forward. He's running like he never has before, stretched and sleek, his tail flying like a bright silver-white flag. Maybe he is Pegasus, after all.

Fosca's great head is dropping behind us. A nanosecond later, we're crossing the finish. Someone is screaming. I think it's me!

"You *star*!" I praise him, reining him in and turning him in a victory circle. Sam whinnies and stamps, tossing his mane, showing off, which makes the crowd laugh. He treats us all to a burst of his song, ending with a loud snort.

"You should enter him for *Idol*," suggests a man behind the ropes. "We could do with the help."

"In first place, with Samphire, Miss Jodie Palmer," announces the loudspeaker. A race official directs me to approach Mr. Lynton, who is holding a trophy and an envelope. Samphire frisks and sidesteps prettily. Somewhere nearby, a band has struck up, and I could swear Sam is moving in time to the music.

"Very well done," says Mr. Lynton. "That was a fine race. Congratulations to you and your splendid horse." He gives me the silver trophy and I shake his hand. The crowd applauds and I lean forward and give Sam the biggest hug ever.

"And I'm delighted to award you a check for one thousand dollars," Mr. Lynton announces. "That should keep Samphire in treats for a little while!" There is laughter and more applause. As I take the silver-edged envelope, my hand is shaking and there are tears of happiness stinging my eyes. It feels like a dream, except I'm aching and stiff and Sam is covered in sweat and dust.

"Thank you so much," I answer. A photographer is taking pictures of us. He doesn't need to ask me to smile. I've realized I'll be able to treat Mom and Ed to a special celebration now. And it's all thanks to Samphire.

We wait while Fosca and the hunter are awarded second- and third-place prizes. Sam nickers when Fosca walks past us. It sounds like a greeting of respect. The gelding looks like a warhorse. He towers above Mr. Lynton.

Mom, Ed, and Rachel are waiting to greet us—I can see them waving like crazy from behind the rope barrier. There's something I have to do first. I dismount and feel in my jacket pocket for Sam's favorite treat—a peppermint.

"You deserve this," I say in his ear. Sam's nose moves over my hand, searching out the sweet. When his tongue finds it, his throat rumbles with pleasure.

Two seconds later, we're both enveloped in a crazy group hug, instigated by Ed and Mom. It gets bigger and crazier as Poppy, Rachel, and the crowd from the stables join in.

"You don't look like a stick in those clothes," observes Ed. I think that's a compliment.

"You're amazing, both of you," says Mom, emotional and giggly at the same time.

"Not me," I reply, pointing to the real star of the show and giving him a kiss between his eyes.

"Excuse me," says a deep voice close by. We all turn to see a man of about forty in a smart tweed suit, approaching. I recognize him as one of the judges from a previous event and wonder if he's going to tell me that there's been some mistake—that Samphire isn't the winner after all. My grip on my trophy tightens a little.

"Bernard Ashton-Cook," he says, offering his firm handshake in introduction to Mom first and then to me. "I was one of the race officials today and I wanted to say how impressed I was with your performance, young lady." His eyes rest on me. They are smiling but cool at the same time.

"Thank you," I respond, unsure what else to say.

"I'm also on the lookout for new additions to my eventing team and wondered if Samphire might, at some point, be for sale? I think he could go all the way, with the right development."

I'm a little taken aback by this. Does he think I'm just a kid playing around at being an owner? That I don't have the expertise or commitment to let Sam reach his full potential? I see that Mom is holding her breath.

"He's not for sale," I state simply.

"I would give you eight thousand dollars. It's a generous offer. I think it reflects his future potential as an event winner. You could buy a nice little horse for that. Stallions aren't for young girls," says Ashton-Cook, eyes hardly blinking. I can tell he's used to wheeling and dealing and getting his way.

"Samphire's part Arab and he'll be worth that just as a sire, let alone as an event horse," I respond. "Even if you offered me a million dollars, the answer would be the same." I turn away and busy myself unstrapping Sam's girth. I sense that the man is appealing to Mom's sensibility in a gesture, inviting her to take his side.

"Jodie's given you her decision," says Mom coolly. "Now, if you'll excuse us, we're taking Samphire home for a family celebration."

"If she should change her mind, here's my card," he informs her, his tone much less friendly. He turns to look at me.

"I won't," I state, holding his gaze. Mom declines his card. He turns and strides away, very disgruntled.

"That was a rude dude," observes Ed before he's out of earshot. Samphire gives a short, sharp whinny in agreement.

Chapter Forty

Hooves thundering across sand, glinting in sunlight, galloping free across the wide sweep of the sun-washed bay. The taste of the ocean in the tears squeezing from my eyes, trickling to my lips. The ripple of muscle against thigh as maximum bareback speed is breached. And behind, the sky; a flaming pink and orange watercolor through the salt-spray in our wake.

Three years ago, it was Dad who was setting the pace, challenging me to raise my skills, take risks, and outride him if I could. Today, I'm racing my very own part-Arab stallion, who has changed my world and rescued me, Mom, and Ed from our isolated island. Even though our opponent is missing four legs and has the added advantage of wings, Samphire is proving a worthy match.

I think Dad would approve, especially as the gleaming Spitfire in my line of sight was presented to Ed in recognition of his selflessness and bravery by Dad's very own squadron.

When I glance over my shoulder, I can see the small figure of Ed, his remote control in his hands, probably wishing he had a red button that says "turbo power" on it—and that he hadn't bet me five dollars that his plane could outperform my excellent horse.

Somewhere near Ed, lying on our picnic rug watching the proceedings, is Mom, looking radiant and relaxed and more at peace than I ever remember.

Our finishing post, the rocky pinnacle of stone that juts out of the sand like a finger at the end of the bay, is about thirty yards away. It's time to let Samphire set the pace. He accelerates just as Ed's Spitfire performs a loop-the-loop in the sky behind us.

"Go, boy, go!" I exclaim, as Sam's shoes splash through the shallow rivulets of incoming tide and I hear the Spitfire gaining ground. I imagine Ed sitting at its controls in the cockpit, the rock in the center of his sights. "Fly, Sam," I urge and my horse responds, lengthening his stride, pushing through the wind with every muscle, every ounce of energy.

We are galloping and I sense Sam's joy in his speed, which is leaving a trail of spray mist suspended in the air. His movement is even more fluid and assured without a saddle. We're running free and it's the best feeling ever.

Suddenly, I notice we have company. The plane has drawn level with us and, in less than five seconds, we reach the rock together. I'm laughing out loud as the Spitfire waggles its wings before soaring vertically toward the sun. And just in case past and present are merging for a moment and the wind can carry words across the shifting space of time, I yell at the top of my voice, "We made it, Dad. Yeeeeeha!"

Acknowledgments

I'd like to thank my American publisher, Albert Whitman & Company, and my US editors, Kristin Ostby and Kristin Zelazko, for giving Samphire the chance to gallop across the States. My thanks, as ever, to all at my UK publisher, Egmont, especially my editor Ali Dougal, Victoria Berwick and the PR team, and designer Emma Eldridge; to my agents, Jodie Marsh and Jane Willis at United Agents. And to Chris, Maddy, and Henry, always.

About the Author

Born in Brighton, England, Jill Hucklesby gained an Honors degree in English and Drama before working in theater, journalism, and as a publicity consultant for arts and medical organizations, including Great Ormond Street Hospital. She lives near the sea in East Sussex with her family and Henry, the unruly retriever.